# FiOnN
#### AND THE
## FiANNa

*For Frances and our own little band of warriors:*
*Esme, Arthur & Patrick.*

Small Kid, Big Legend

# FiOnN
## AND FiAnNa
## THE

# RONAN MOORE
### ILLUSTRATED BY ALEXANDRA COLOMBO

*Gill Books*

Gill Books
Hume Avenue
Park West
Dublin 12
www.gillbooks.ie

Gill Books is an imprint of M.H. Gill and Co.

978 0717191000

Edited by Emma Dunne.
Proofread by Jane Rogers.
Designed by iota (www.iota-books.ie).

Printed by CPI Group (UK) Ltd,
Croydon CR0 4YY
This book is typeset in IM Fell.

The paper used in this book comes from
the wood pulp of managed forests. For
every tree felled, at least one tree is planted,
thereby renewing natural resources.

A CIP catalogue record for this book is
available from the British Library.

5 4 3 2 1

# CONTENTS

# HOW TO PRONOUNCE THE NAMES IN THIS BOOK

| | |
|---:|:---|
| Abcán | Ow-cawn |
| Áed | Ay *or* Ee |
| Ailill | Al-lil |
| Art | Art |
| Artúir | Art-oo-wir |
| Benandonner | Ban-an-doh-ner |
| Benne | Ben-ye |
| Berrach Brecc | Bar-akh Brack |
| Bodb Derg | Byve Jar-ug |
| Boladh | Boll-u |
| Caicer | Ky-khayr |

| | |
|---|---|
| Cailte | Kweel-tche |
| Cál Crodae | Caul Crow-ga |
| Cana | Con-na |
| Cearbhall | Car-ool |
| Cernunnos | Cor-non-ass |
| Cnes | Knass *or* Krass |
| Conan | Cun-awn |
| Conbec | Cun-weg *or* Cun-veg |
| Connla | Cunn-lah |
| Covey | Coo-vee |
| Créde | Cree-gah |
| Crimmal | Crim-oll |
| Cumhall | Coo-al or Cool |
| Dagda | Jaw-yee-ah |
| Dealra Dubh | Jawl-ra Duv |

| | |
|---|---|
| Dianras | Jean-riss |
| Diorraing | Jur-ing |
| Donn | Dhun *or* Dhown |
| Échna | Ag-ne |
| Eitne Ollamda | Eth-nye Oll-oon-ta |
| Eochaid Feidlech | Och-ee File-och |
| Ernamis | Air-nah-mish |
| Feargach | Far-goch |
| Fedlimid | Fail-im-ee |
| Fiacha | Fee-ack-ha |
| Finnegas | Finn-ay-gus |
| Fionn | F-yun *or* Finn |
| Foltor | Full-tore |
| Fuaim | Foo-imm |
| Goll | Gull |

| | |
|---|---|
| Iollan | Ull-an |
| Lachtna | Lough-na |
| Lombhall | Lum-woll |
| Luas | Loo-as |
| Lugach | Loo-ee |
| Manannán | Monn-a-nawn |
| Morna | More-na |
| Ossnat | Us-nit |
| Raigne | Roy-neah |
| Rian (chief) | Ree-an |
| Ros | Russ |
| Sadb | Syve |
| Saothar | Say-her |
| Sárait | Saw-rit |
| Searbhann Lochlann | Shar-van Lough-lan |

| | |
|---|---|
| Steallaire | Shtal-era |
| Suileach | Soo-wi-lough |
| Tadg | Thighg |
| Trénmor | Thrain-woor |
| Úaine | OOih-nye |

# THE REBIRTH OF THE FIANNA

There was a knock at the door.

'Fionn, you here?'

A mop of corn-gold hair poked out from behind a screen. 'Hi, Cana — just give me a moment.'

'How are you feeling?' she called to him.

'Nervous. Excited. Sad that my parents won't be there beside me. Glad that you and the others will.'

'Sure, what else would we be doing? Now step out and let's have a look at you.'

Fionn viewed his reflection in the mirror, a polished disc of bronze hanging from the wall. Though he was not yet fourteen, already the definition of a man was beginning to form. His shoulders had broadened in the last year and his chest had started to become more pronounced. His clothes that once hung lightly from his body were now being filled out with muscle. And in the last few months alone, he had grown several inches. Though he would be no giant, from his shape, stature and poise it was already clear that this soon-to-be young man would be a warrior like no other.

'How do I look?'

'Clean!' She laughed. 'I'll leave you to finish getting ready and will see you out there.'

'Thanks ... and ...' Cana stopped and turned to listen. Her short brown hair framed a striking face of olive complexion. 'You're a good friend.'

'And you're going to be late for the High King.' She smiled. 'So hurry up.'

Fionn, son of Cumhall, lay down on his bed and collected his thoughts. It was a big day. Little over a week ago, he had arrived at the royal capital of Tara with a volunteer force of young men and women. He had come to stake his claim to be the head of the Fianna, its rightful champion. It was a role that his father, Cumhall, had held for several years before it was taken from him because he had chosen to elope with Fionn's mother, Muirne. The title had been passed instead to one-eyed Áed 'Goll' Mac Morna, a monstrous individual who had later killed Fionn's father in battle and then sought to find and murder Fionn for the first thirteen years of his life. However, Fionn had not been found.

He had come to Tara seeking justice. What he'd found, however, was a city in turmoil, under siege from a dragon, and a High King and people who needed help. It was he, Fionn Mac Cumhaill, not Goll, who answered the king's call and slew the dragon. And it was Fionn who was now being rewarded with the leadership of the Fianna.

'Fionn, get a move on,' a girl's voice came from outside. 'If you don't hurry up, they might end up making Iollan the champion instead!'

'Shut up, will you?' came the response of a boy.

Fionn smiled. They were the unmistakable voices of Cnes and Iollan. He had fought alongside Cnes down south against an unearthly beast that had threatened her community. Iollan he had met when hurling up north. They were always needling each other, with Cnes usually the instigator of their humorous arguments. It was Iollan's younger sister, Cana, though, whom Fionn was closest to. She had taught him to hurl and taken him in as one of her own. With his parents dead, these three were the closest thing to family Fionn had, and he was grateful for that.

It was these three who were among the first to answer his call to arms and to rise up against a Fianna that had largely become corrupt since his father had left. And it was these three who had shared some of the happiest moments in recent times, even while being hunted by the forces of Goll Mac Morna. Thinking of Goll made Fionn momentarily shiver. A part of him had hoped that Goll would not accept the High King's decision to strip him of his captaincy and deliver it to Fionn. And they would have settled it, not with the wrestling match by which his father and others before him had won the title, but with swords. But Goll had not given him that satisfaction and instead had taken the troops loyal to him and fled overseas, swearing revenge. One day he would return and Fionn and the Fianna would have to be ready, but not today. Today was a time to celebrate.

With the High King of Ireland – Conn of the Hundred Battles – facing him on the royal seat, Fionn got down on one knee as Caicer the Chief Druid placed a sword gently upon his head. It was the signal for Fionn to begin.

'I, Fionn, son of Cumhall and Muirne, swear to be peaceable in a great man's house; be hardy in the wilderness; avoid the fool in battle; and not mock the holy man, nor be involved in quarrels.

'I swear to keep well away from these two, the witch and the evil man; be kind to poets, makers of art and to the common soldiery; and not take the best seat away from friends and advisers; not boast, nor offer what I cannot rightly give; and not forsake my king for as long as I live.

'I swear to keep from gossip and lies; not be unkind to an old man; heed words of good counsel; be a listener in the forest, a watcher on the plain; and be alert to the enemy of Ireland.

'I swear not to be mean with food or be a miser's friend; not to speak ill of great men; and always have my armour and weapons ready for the outbreak of sudden battle.

'For gold, silver or wealth, I will not betray my promise.'

'Then rise, Fionn,' said the High King, 'Champion of the Fianna'.

That evening, Tara feasted. Never had a banquet been prepared that pleased men and women more. Eight-score vats of fine nectar, mead and ale, from the best of every fruit, honeycomb, malt and wort. Plates of venison, boar, beef and rabbit adorned with every root vegetable the season could supply. Doormen, cupbearers and carvers of meat were there to serve the High King and the court, Fionn, his friends and supporters and the rest of the Fianna. Spigots were set in the great vats of dark yew, jars of bronze and dishes of gold and silver were set on the tables, and all were soon furnished with food and drink as minstrels and musicians played dulcimers, harps, bagpipes and flutes.

Amid this night-time cheer, Conn the High King felt a deep pang of regret as he observed his new champion. It had been Goll who had given the deathly blow to Fionn's father all those years ago at the Battle of Cnucha. However, Conn knew his blood was also on that sword. He was the king, the High King of Ireland, and Cumhall had helped him gain and hold this role through many of the hundred battles of his fame. Yet he had failed his old friend. All because Cumhall had run away and married Muirne, daughter of Tadg, who had then held the role of Chief Druid. In doing so, he had broken a rule that champions of the Fianna should not marry. But this rule had been a recent one. It had been brought in to prevent bloodshed, not to cause it. But Conn had allowed the anger and betrayal he'd felt at Cumhall's departure to blind him. He had chosen to listen to Tadg, who had a wicked thirst for revenge. He had not realised that the Chief Druid had grown corrupt and become consumed with hate, possessed by an evil Otherworldly spirit known as the Dealra Dubh — one of the Tuatha Dé Danann, a supernatural race that had once lived in Ireland, long before the first people arrived. There were many types of Tuatha, spirits and gods, but the Dealra Dubh was one that wished only death and suffering on the living. By the time Conn had realised his mistake, it was too late. Cumhall had been killed. In the years that followed, Conn's regret and growing weakness had allowed his kingdom, and the Fianna who helped rule it, to deteriorate.

At least he had rid himself of Tadg, sending him out into the wilderness with just the clothes on his back. And Conn had ensured that his only child, Art, was mentored by someone of greater character, a man by the name of Fiacha — a true and honourable warrior of the Fianna. Art had grown into a worthy young man. He sought counsel and showed leadership in equal measure. He cared for those around him no matter what their status and understood that respect was earned through modelling leadership, not generating fear. And though Art may not have had the fighting skills of his father, Conn thought he would make a wiser leader, who would be led by both head and heart.

Conn knew that it was time. Not only should the Fianna have a new leader, so too should Ireland.

'Men and women,' he declared, rising from his royal seat, 'warriors and followers of our new champion, Fionn. I want to first raise a drinking horn to Fionn Mac Cumhaill. Without him we would not be sitting here. And I have no doubt that under his guidance the Fianna will thrive once more. To Fionn! A new champion, a new leader. One who I am sure will inspire hope, command loyalty and keep us safe, something that we have lacked for a long time now. As king, I know that I have let my people down these past years.' Silence fell as Conn took a breath, searching for the right words. 'This, I promise, will change. And this change will begin tonight. When I look at Fionn, I understand that youth must be given its chance. So, having watched my only child grow to become a man, I announce tonight that we will have a new king. I will pass on my crown to my son, Art Mac Cuinn, our next High King of Ireland!'

A month later, crowds, much larger this time, again gathered in the Royal Hall — this time for a coronation. In the hall, Art stepped up onto a standing stone known as the Lia Fáil. As he did, the ground rumbled and a shriek emanated from the rock — a sign the people took to mean that the gods were satisfied with this choice.

But in the night that followed Art's coronation, Fionn did not rest well. A thought disturbed his sleep, a thought he needed to share.

'Art and I are a new start for both Ireland and the Fianna,' he said to Cana, Cnes and Iollan the next morning. 'People want their High King and their Fianna to look after them, to keep them safe. But I am not sure if we are ready or convinced we can protect them, not yet anyway. And not if Goll returns with a foreign force behind him.'

'What do you propose?' Cana asked.

Fionn bit his thumb. Ever since he had burned it on the legendary Salmon of Knowledge, insight had often flooded to him when he bit it. As he held the thumb in his mouth, inspiration arrived. 'We need to relearn the skills that made the Fianna a force respected the world over.'

'How will we do that?' said Cnes.

'I know every poem that tells us what we need to do. All we need is someone who remembers these old ways and can train us. And I know just the man.'


'Oh yes, I remember how we trained back in the day. For months, from dawn to dusk, we learned how to be true Fianna warriors,' Fionn's uncle Crimmal recalled over breakfast.

'And sometimes all through the night,' added his old friend Fiacha.

Crimmal nodded. 'Yes, night and day. We would have breakfast the evening before so not to waste time come morning.'

'And let's not forget dinner in the morning to keep us going through the day.'

'But,' Fionn interrupted, 'do you remember the old skills well enough to teach them?'

'I think we do,' Crimmal said, scratching his beard. 'What do you think, Fiacha?'

His friend nodded in agreement.

'Yes.' Crimmal said. 'Have the dinner ready for us first thing tomorrow morning, Fionn, and we'll begin.'

Early the next morning, Crimmal and Fiacha were ready – they had eaten their dinner and dressed in their finest warrior gear. Each had a tunic, cloak and trousers, brightly dyed with local berries and lichens and held together with a thick leather belt. Such was their seriousness about the training, they had even painted large parts of their arms and faces with the blue of the woad plant, rarely done except for battle.

'Looking good, uncle,' Fionn said, somewhat surprised at Crimmal's warlike appearance.

'You don't think I've gone overboard? It's been a while since I've got painted up.'

'No, not at all. You look ... terrifying.'

'Great. That's what I was going for.'

In front of them were nearly a hundred young faces. All these people wanted to be not just soldiers but elite warriors of the Fianna.

As Crimmal studied his class, he noticed almost two dozen young women among those present. 'Er ... Fionn?'

'What's wrong?' Fionn asked, stepping away from the group so all would not hear.

'Well, this is where we begin our training to become members of the Fianna.'

'I know. I was there last night when we discussed this.'

'Yes, but ...' Crimmal paused a moment. 'There are women here.'

'Well spotted, Uncle. I am glad the face paint hasn't affected your vision. What's the problem?'

'It's just that the Fianna is an all-male fighting force.'

'Says who?'

'Er ... em ... I don't know, Fionn. It's just how I remember it.'

'Hmmm.' Fionn pondered, biting his thumb as he turned to the new recruits standing patiently in front of them in lines ten abreast. Fionn then nodded towards two women at the end of the nearest line. 'That's Ernamis and Échna. They're twin sisters, although you wouldn't think it as Ernamis is nearly a foot taller. They grew up on the Western Isles of Aran. When the sisters were just sixteen, their parents' boat was boarded by pirates who robbed and killed all aboard. Though hardly adults, they took over the running of their parents' land and surrounding seas. They then hunted down those pirates, who had continued raiding and killing up and down the coast. Ernamis was already nearly six feet at that stage, and she bludgeoned her way through half the crew. Her sister, Échna, an expert with the skene dagger, filleted her parents' murderer, sending him to the bottom of the ocean as seafood. Ernamis loves embroidery, by the way.

'Behind them is Úaine, standing beside her cousin Raigne the Wide-Eyed. Úaine is daughter of Fíal, son of Dub from the Fanad Peninsula up north, a family known for generosity across this island. One day, a neighbouring clan took advantage of that generosity and plundered their food stores, killing her father and their grandfather. Úaine led her clan to retake what was theirs. She was equally generous in that she chose not to take the heads of those who had slain her kin but sent them back to be buried alongside their bodies. And five people to her left is Sárait.'

'Who were her parents?'

'I don't know. No one does. They were aboard a trading ship from the vast searing hot lands to our south. The ship was blown off course in a storm. She was the only person to survive. Still a baby, she was pulled from the waves by Eochaid Feidlech. He had heard the calls of help in his sleep and had led a search party into the storm. He is her foster father now.'

'Eochaid Feidlech?' Crimmal asked, surprised. 'Eochaid the Enduring?'

'Yes,' Fionn answered. 'The same one who killed twenty well-armed Lochlann invaders with his bare hands when already in his sixties. Well, he has grown old now and feels she needs to learn some discipline because he thinks her too fierce!'

'Too fierce?'

'Yes, too fierce. They say she can pick a fight in an empty room.'

'And, er, what of the woman standing two rows behind her?'

'Which one?' Fionn asked.

'The young woman whose height doesn't reach the shoulder of the recruit beside her and who walks with a limp.'

'Ah, you must mean little Ossnat? From a very poor family in the midlands, she is an incredible tracker. Despite her limp, she is capable of stalking almost anything in the wild. And when it comes to putting an arrow into the eye of an enemy from a dozen ridges away, few can match her. Now, I know of no poems that the great poet Finnegas taught me that said women could not be in the Fianna. And many of these young women are here because they want the Fianna to make the island a safer, more secure and more peaceful place. But if you want to tell any of them they are not welcome, be my guest.'

Crimmal looked at Fionn and then back over at all the recruits. 'Right, everybody, you're all very welcome to our first day of training. Today we will begin with basic weaponry. Hands up if you have ever used a sword, spear, dart, javelin, battle-axe, hand-axe, sling, bow and arrow, skene or dagger?'

At the end of their first week of lessons, Crimmal set the would-be recruits their first test. Simply completing the training was not enough; to become a member of the Fianna, each recruit had to pass a series of tests that had been laid down for generations. The first one was being able to extend one's arm and hold a javelin by the handle end without it quivering for the length of time it took to boil a cauldron of water, and then to cast the javelin accurately at a target nine ridges away. Every day they had practised. Some were masters of the spear and easily passed the test. Cál Crodae was one. He wielded a charmed spear named the Brave and Quick Wounding. It was said that it never missed its mark and any man who was bloodied by it would die within nine days. Cnes, whose accuracy with the spear was well known, also passed immediately. As did Fionn, who, though younger than everyone else, had a level of skill with each weapon that few could surpass.

When the test ended, all but a few had succeeded. On the sideline, a druid looked on. Crimmal drew Fionn's attention to him. 'It seems like the Chief Druid wants to speak to you.'

14

Seeing Fionn frown, his uncle continued, 'Caicer is as different from your grandfather Tadg as night is from day. You can trust him.'

From behind a table of clutter laden with liquids and pastes, the skeletal bodies of woodland animals and insects, and a sea of accoutrements, curios and curiosities, Fionn could hear rustling and see the faint glow of candlelight. 'Druid Caicer, you wanted to see me?' Fionn enquired.

Poking his head up, Caicer rose to his feet as quickly as his seventy-odd years would allow. 'I wondered if you would honour me with a visit. But then I got tired of waiting and thought I'd invite you here myself.'

'I'm sorry. I suppose I was —'

'Thinking I would be like your grandfather?' Caicer said, finishing his thought. 'I understand. I would be wary of druids after hearing stories of Tadg. But then should we be wary of the champions of the Fianna because of the likes of Goll?'

Fionn nodded. 'Do you know where he is now?'

'Goll or Tadg?' said Caicer. 'If it is Goll, I have only heard rumours that he is on the island of Albion, to our east. As for your grandfather Tadg, no one knows. It was a mistake for the High King to allow him to leave with his head still on his shoulders. He was last seen crossing the great Shannon river one dark, cloudless night. However, over the years that followed there were many reports of a malevolent old man of druid-like appearance who helped thieves and brigands open up sidhe mounds.'

'These sidhes are the same type of portals to the Otherworld that the dragon emerged from?'

'Yes, and many monsters have been released that the Fianna will have to deal with in time. These sidhe mounds were shut not just with stone and boulders but also with magic. Many also contained gold and silver, which were offerings to the gods. When the thieves and brigands removed the rocks to access the treasure, Tadg used whatever remained of his powers to open the magical seals.'

'Why?'

'To cause trouble? To seek revenge? I don't really know.'

'But Art told me he has no more powers. He left with nothing: neither sacred texts of sorcery nor the Chief Druid's staff,' Fionn said, nodding at a stick that stood behind Caicer. It was some six foot in length, and at its top was the Bóinne Mace Head, a decorative ball of solid flint that conferred great power on those who knew how to wield it.

'Yes, you're right — we took back the staff. But of the three sacred texts of the druids, the Great Book of

Moytura, perhaps the most powerful of the three and which contained tracts of dark magic, was never found. However, the truth is that druids always have power, and you underestimate them at your peril. That is why in the palace of Almu, which Tadg had built and was expelled from, a garrison of soldiers is stationed in case he were to return. But I didn't ask you here to talk about him. I wanted to show you something.' Caicer lifted up a magnificent-looking bronze instrument that at first looked like an S-shaped staff with a mouthpiece on one end and a larger opening in the shape of a boar's head on the other.

'What is it?' Fionn asked, marvelling at its craft.

'It's a type of horn, a carnyx called a Dord Fiann. We have a number of them. In earlier times, they were used to call people to the support of the High King and the Fianna, to warn of invasions, sound battle and give instructions in the heat of conflict. As you revitalise the Fianna, I think they will prove very useful.'

'Right, this morning we will begin focusing on defence,' Crimmal said. 'Remember, you can't attack properly if you've just had your arm cut off!'

'Or your leg,' said Fiacha.

'Indeed,' Crimmal replied. 'Basically, if you want to be an effective warrior you need all parts of your body to stay attached. So, for the next round of training, Fiacha here is going to help you learn the true art of defence and prevent you from getting killed.'

'Thank you Crimmal,' Fiacha began. 'Now, Donn and Lugach have agreed to be our first two volunteers. Surrounding each of them are nine warriors and recruits stationed a distance of nine furrows away. Using a staff and shield, they will need to fend off every missile cast at them. Today we'll start with hazelnuts, acorns and pine cones.'

Donn, who was the brawn to Lugach's brain, and who hadn't recalled volunteering, asked, 'Why are you using nuts?'

Ten minutes later, and nursing many quickly rising welts and swellings, he had his answer.

'We are using nuts first,' Fiacha answered, 'because they hurt a lot less than the knives, darts, spears and javelins we'll throw at you when you're ready!'

After Fiacha had finished training and testing the recruits in the art of defence, Crimmal began the art of evasion. One group of recruits had to outrun another through the forest with only ten spear lengths of a head start. They had to not only maintain their lead but also defend themselves against any assaults from their pursuers, as well as overcome obstacles at speed, such as leaping over a downed breast-high tree trunk and passing under a bough no higher than their knee. And should a thorn pierce their foot, they had to be able to take it out without breaking their stride!

While Fionn, Cana and Donn were known to be the fastest of the Fianna, most recruits were still confident that they could maintain a lead over their fellows. Others, though, were less sure. One of those was Diorraing. Despite his baby face, he was all of 6 foot 8 inches and weighed 20 stone, much of which was muscle. While he was strong as an oak, he didn't move quickly. And when he saw how swiftly the likes of Donn could cover ground with long, loping strides, he felt nervous. Looking out over the course that Crimmal had set up, Diorraing could only visualise failure.

'What are you looking at?' came a soft voice from behind. Diorraing turned to see the wren-like figure of Ossnat approaching him with the slight but discernible limp that defined her gait. Beside her walked Úaine and Raigne.

'Defeat,' Diorraing answered, 'I am looking at defeat.'

'What does defeat look like?' she asked.

'There is no way I will be able to keep ahead of the others through this forest. And when I fall behind, my time as a recruit of the Fianna will come to an end. Why? What do you see when you look out across here?'

'I see another challenge that I will have to overcome,' Ossnat said. 'Just like every other challenge I've had to overcome in my life. Yet here I am. And next week I expect to still be here, as should you. Look, when I was younger, I had no family to look after me. I spent my time knocking on doors, asking to come in, to be included, to play with others. And most of the time that door never opened. That left me with a choice: I could leave or ...'

'Or what?' Diorraing asked.

'Or I could climb in the window.' She smiled. 'And I've been climbing in the window ever since.'

There was a moment of silence between them as Diorraing suddenly felt a little awkward in his 6-foot-8-inch skin. 'I don't think I would have fit through the window,' he said. 'I'd have broken the door down.'

'I'm sure you would!' Ossnat laughed, putting Diorraing at ease. 'We'd make a great team. But this isn't a door that we can break down or a window we can climb through. It's a course we must navigate and that is what we are here to do. Why not join us and learn the course, and that way your guile will help your speed.'

'Why are you two here?' Diorraing asked Raigne and Úaine. 'Surely you'll be able to manage this?'

Raigne grinned. 'I'm sure Úaine will. She just came along for company. Me, though, I need to do some homework. I might be known as the Wide-Eyed but I'm blind in one eye with poor vision in the other.'

'What?' Diorraing said. 'But I saw you defend yourself from nine of us with ease only a few days ago?'

'I did,' Raigne replied. 'But my ears alerted me to your throws as much as my limited vision. And I was standing still, which always helps. This isn't as easy and that's why I am here.'

That evening and the ones that followed, they walked and ran the course, familiarising themselves not only with each bush, branch and tree trunk but also with the contours of the woodland floor, how it took a foot and the obstacles they had to overcome. While both Diorraing and Ossnat improved hugely in speed, Raigne's gains were not as marked, though it didn't seem to worry him.

The end of the week came quickly and, with it, the test. All through the day, recruits took turns as either chaser or quarry. No quarter was given and as the day wore on many recruits failed. Of course, when someone fell short and saw their chance of becoming a Fianna warrior disappear, others gave comfort. Though one recruit did not. A young man by the name of Lachtna felt no pity for those who missed out and was gleeful when it was he who caught a recruit and ended their chances. It was a trait that others disliked, though it bothered Lachtna little.

Of the trio, Ossnat's turn came first and, as she predicted, by the end of it she was still a Fianna recruit, having lost little of the head start each runner was given. Diorraing gave up even less, which only left Raigne. It was well into the evening when it was finally his turn, but Raigne first had a question. 'In the rules of this test, does it say when this chase needs to happen?'

'No,' replied Crimmal, 'just the distance and the number of pursuers.'

'Well,' Raigne replied, 'if it's okay, I'd like to wait another hour before my turn.'

'But it will be dark at that stage. How will you see?'

'I'll see as well as those pursuing me,' Raigne said confidently.

An hour later Raigne's chosen pursuers tripped, stumbled and fell in the night-time darkness of the forest. Lachtna was among them, doing his best to catch Raigne. But the only thing he caught was the trunk of a pine tree, splitting his lip open and knocking himself near unconscious, something that brought a degree of satisfaction to the others. Meanwhile, Raigne let his feet guide him and not only maintained his lead but lengthened it and passed with flying colours.

Autumn gave way to winter and a slowly reducing number of recruits faced and overcame tasks that ranged from swimming and climbing to hiding and throwing. And much to Fionn's delight, his closest friends — Cnes, Iollan and Cana — hung in there. What any of them might have lacked in experience, they all made up for in determination and practice. Throughout this time, they trained in the art of war during the day and studied poetry at night — a key skill for any warrior, so they could not only learn and pass on verses of knowledge and history but also compose their own.

By the first shoots of spring, Crimmal and Fiacha had completed their teaching and the remaining recruits stood in front of them as the new Fianna. They were ready to join those past warriors who had stayed loyal to the High King and not fled with Goll.

Both Crimmal and Fiacha looked at them with pride. Cana, Cnes and Iollan. Diorraing, Ossnat, Úaine and her cousin Raigne. Sisters Échna and Ernamis. Eitne Ollamda the Learned, whose knowledge of magic and healing was thought to rival even that of the Chief Druid but whose sword-play was altogether stronger. Best friends Donn and Lugach. The great singer and storyteller Cailte Mac Ronan and the spear-thrower Cál Crodae. Sárait, who had yet to become any less fierce, and Lachtna, who had yet to become any less unpleasant.

'Nearly fifty of us started,' Iollan proudly whispered to Cnes, 'and now only fifteen of us remain. Like a hurling team.'

'Actually, sixteen of us,' Cnes whispered back as she nodded across at Lachtna, who, to her disappointment, had easily passed the final test. 'What position would you give him on your hurling team?'

'Left back.'

'Left back?' Cnes asked.

'Yes, left back in the woods unconscious.'

As they giggled, the High King and Fionn approached.

'Well done, Fionn,' Art said to his champion as he reviewed the new warriors.

'Thank you, High King. We now have a fighting force worthy of their name.'

'Indeed. And now it is time to win back the trust of every person who lives on this island.'

'Any ideas how we should start?' Fionn asked.

The High King smiled. 'Have you ever heard of the Piast of Loch Cuan?'

# THE MONSTERS OF THE SiDHE

Inside the Royal Hall, the High King, Fionn, Crimmal, Cana, Cnes, Iollan and the Chief Druid, Caicer, were in deep discussion.

'So, this Piast is some sort of water serpent?' said Fionn.

'Yes,' said Art. 'If we had heard such stories years ago, we would have thought little of it – drunken tales told by those who wanted to entertain. But we have all seen beasts that have defied explanation in recent years.'

'Like the dragon,' said Cana.

'Exactly,' Art replied.

'And you think the Piast has come from a sidhe? One of the underground portals to the Otherworld that Tadg has helped to open?' said Fionn.

'Yes,' said Caicer, 'I believe so. There are a lot of these sidhes around the island, and we have heard many reports of local clans and villages successfully fighting back against smaller Otherworldly creatures that had threatened them — something the Fianna should have been doing. But there are a few, like the Piast of Loch Cuan, that have wreaked real havoc.'

'How many, exactly?'

'We think five,' Caicer said as he rolled out a long parchment.

'What is this?' Fionn asked, his eyes widening.

'It's vellum, the skin of a calf.'

'I know what vellum is,' said Fionn. 'But what on earth is marked on it?'

'Oh!' Caicer smiled. 'This is the island of Ireland.'

'Aren't we standing on the island of Ireland?' asked Iollan, a little perplexed.

'We are, but this is the island at a much smaller scale. We call it a map.

'We got this from a fisherman who had taken it from a visiting trading boat. All of Ireland's important places are on it.'

Cnes butted in. 'Where are the kingdoms of Kerry?'

'There.' Caicer pointed at the very edge of the country.

'I thought you said it was for important places,' Iollan said, smiling teasingly at Cnes, who flicked a rosehip she was eating at his head. 'Ow!'

Caicer proceeded to explain the map in more detail. He pointed out Tara first and then the other significant sites on the island, before identifying where the five worst monsters of the sidhe had been spotted.

When Caicer finished, Fionn looked at the High King. 'What do you suggest we do?'

'We act,' Art said. 'The Fianna are ready. You are ready. The people need a force that they know can protect them once more. We all know that threats lie overseas, and one day Goll Mac Morna and his men will return — and with them will come many others to try to defeat us. It could be this year or next year or the year after. The truth is, we don't know. But what we do know is that there are dangers among us right now — these monsters of the sidhe. If we are to win back the hearts and minds of our people, we need to deal with them. And when we do, we will help the locals cover these sidhes and Caicer and our druids will seal them shut once more.'

By sunrise the next morning, Fionn was already addressing his fellow Fianna warriors.

'While Crimmal will remain with a body of warriors in Tara, the rest of us will divide up and take the five roads out: Cál, Diorraing and Ossnat to the south-east; Cnes, Iollan, Échna and Ernamis down to Munster; Eitne, Úaine, Raigne and Lachtna into the midlands; Cana, Cailte and Sárait west to Connacht; and I will lead Donn and Lugach northwards to Ulster. We are all tasked with dealing with monsters that are terrorising the heart and each corner of this island. Go with luck and come back safe.'

Of the groups that set out, it was Cál, Diorraing and Ossnat in the south-east who first met their target. In the Wicklow Mountains, in an area known as the Ford of the Slaney, there was a hamlet of huts that once had been rich with life. Now it lay almost empty. A farmer named Coscrach was one of the few who had remained. Surrounded by his family, he stood in the dark of his empty hovel and told Cál of the curse that had befallen them. For the last four years, whenever it was time to reap their crops on the fertile foothills of these mountains, a herd of deer, led by a white stag whose eyes shone blood red, would come down the slopes. They would destroy everything and kill or maim anyone who dared stand in their way. As a result, many a person had been lost to starvation and disease.

'Deer are skittish and highly strung. They don't attack,' Diorraing said.

'These do,' the old man replied ruefully.

'Coscrach, I know what it is like to grow up hungry through no fault of your own,' said Ossnat. As she bent down to share some food they had brought, she added, 'But fear not, we will enter these mountains, find this herd and your family will not spend another winter like this.'

After several weeks, Ossnat's tracking skills helped to uncover the deer. High in the mountains they found a sidhe and beside it a herd of almost three hundred deer with a white stag holding court in the centre.

'My goodness! That is some herd of deer!' Diorraing said.

'What now?' asked Ossnat. 'Attack?'

'No,' said Cál. 'At best, we'd kill a half-dozen each. And then, a couple of hundred would either overrun us or take off down the mountain into the ripening crops below.'

'Well, we didn't come up here to admire the views,' said Diorraing. 'We need to do something.'

'You're right, but I don't think we need to or even could kill them all. I think we just need to kill that white stag. It seems to have a power over this herd. If we kill it, then it might break that bond.'

'And if it doesn't?' Silence gave Diorraing his answer. 'Great, killed by deer. I'd never live it down!'

Ossnat smiled at Diorraing's remark before speaking. 'Cál, you have the best throw of a spear. On your mark, Diorraing and I will lead an attack and open up as much of a path as we can to give you the clearest shot possible. Just try not to miss.'

A few moments later, a cry went up and Diorraing and Ossnat rushed forward. The deer, though stunned at first, charged back at them. Cál was right. They did slay half a dozen each before it looked like they would be overwhelmed, only for the deer to suddenly stop and dash away in every direction. When the animals disappeared, Diorraing and Ossnat could see the white stag lying dead on the woodland floor, downed by the spear of Cál.

While Cál and his group were preparing to return home following the closing of the sidhe, eighty miles away, in the middle of the country, another band of Fianna were battling to stay alive.

For months, Eitne, Úaine, Raigne and Lachtna had slowly made their way through the central plains. The monster they were tasked to face was rumoured to rest in the depths of Lough Ree. But they had been confronted by and had to defeat several smaller beasts of different shapes and sizes on their way, which had delayed their approach to the vast lake.

Lough Ree was one of the largest bodies of water along the great Shannon river. It had been fished for as long as Ireland had been inhabited, and it had once been a source of life for the local people. But in recent times fishermen had disappeared, and it had become synonymous with death. There were rumours of a monster that lurked deep under the surface, but no one had ever seen it — or survived to tell the tale. No one felt safe on or near the lake and the fishing villages had been abandoned.

In these lake-covered parts of Ireland, birds such as crows and pigeons were often used to send messages. One afternoon, as the band of Fianna were speaking to some farmers several miles from the lake shore, a crow came from across the lake with news. An otter the size of a man had been spotted on the lake's western front, feasting on slaughtered livestock, each of the last three nights. The warriors knew that it would take days to circle the lake, by which time the otter surely would have disappeared. So they chose to travel across the water instead. But shortly after they pushed off from shore, the hunters became the hunted.

They were blind to an aquatic monster, a kraken of sorts, which wrapped its tentacles around the ropes that held their raft together. By the time Úaine felt a strange movement underfoot and sensed danger, it was too late. With a swift, violent tug, the raft was pulled under, sending the warriors into the cold water. Had it not been for their skill as swimmers and the closeness of a small island nearby they would have all surely perished, dragged below and drowned. Instead, they clambered onto the land with few weapons and no options. As the hours passed darkness fell, leaving the motley group to sit shivering together. It was then that the King of the Otters arrived.

'Look out! The monster can walk on land,' Lachtna shouted, drawing his dagger as the otter, as tall as he, approached.

To everyone's surprise, it spoke. 'I am as much a monster as you are. My name is Dobhar-Chú, the King of the Otters, and, unlike that monster that still lies beneath the water, I wish no harm upon you.'

For a moment, the warriors were silent. Then Eitne spoke. 'Yet you are the creature that locals have said has slaughtered and feasted upon their livestock.'

'Yes, I am. This lake monster has killed so many fish that there is little left to feed my family, so I have no option but to find food where I can. But we have a common enemy, and I come here so that we might work together.'

'Work with a talking otter? Never!' Lachtna angrily replied.

'In case you haven't noticed, we are stuck on an island surrounded by water, beneath which a monster lurks,'

Eitne snapped. 'This is not a position of strength. I, for one, would like to hear what the Dobhar-Chú wants to tell us.' To Lachtna's disgust both Raigne and Úaine nodded in agreement. 'So,' Eitne continued, 'how might we work together?'

The King of the Otters began explaining that the monster did not swim the lake waters at night but instead retreated to Loch Fuinseann, a much smaller body of water that had the look of wickedness, many miles to the west. 'The monster's sidhe lies just below the shoreline of that lake, and it rests nightly in the deep pool of water. The water of that lake is fed by Lough Ree through an underground channel. It then flows out through a series of swallet holes on the lake bed, far too narrow for the monster to pass through. As a result it only has one way to get in or out. I can plug the underground channel and the water level will drop. By the time the monster wakes it will be lying vulnerable in the shallows. But you won't have long, because it will try to return through the underground channel to Lough Ree and its strength will surely break the dam that I will create. There is only one thing I ask of you.'

'What?' Eitne asked guardedly.

'The lake that is left behind. I will help breathe life back into Lough Ree, and for that I want the local people to give me and my family free rein of Loch Fuinseann.

Ask the locals to swear they will never fish there, and in return we promise never to disturb the world of men and women again.'

It was a fair deal, and despite Lachtna's dissatisfaction, the word of the Fianna was given. That night the Dobhar-Chú helped ferry them off the island. He also returned to them whatever weapons he could find on the lake floor. The next evening, as planned, the underground channel was dammed. By dawn, the water had dropped, and the Fianna attacked the unsuspecting beast. By the time the sun had completely risen, the Lake Monster of Lough Ree, a cephalopod-like creature with a hundred tentacles, lay dead on what was now the dry lake bed of Loch Fuinseann.

Around them were hundreds upon hundreds of fish — rich pickings for the Dobhar-Chú and his clan of otters who soon arrived. Eitne smiled, realising that the king had secured a treasure trove for his kind. And to this day, when a coronation takes place for a new King of the Otters, that underwater channel is dammed, and once again the otters feast uninterrupted.

While it was a beast from the water that had almost defeated Eitne's band of warriors, for Cnes, Iollan, Échna and Ernamis to the south, danger came from the air.

They travelled to the old Kingdom of Cork. At its southern coast, a vast flock of demonic birds with gnawing beaks and flesh-tearing talons were terrorising villages and settlements.

For several years, the birds had emerged from a sidhe rumoured to be on the Cliffs of Choitín. At first, just like the white stag and his herd, they attacked whatever crops were ready to harvest. But their appetites grew more wicked and soon there were reports of them carrying off small animals and even children. Whole villages had moved away from the cliffs, but the evil flock came further inland.

The Fianna's first skirmishes with these evil birds proved injurious, with not one member escaping without a scratch, cut or gash. Yet, despite these wounds, they had managed to kill only a few dozen birds out of a vast flock.

'What now?' Iollan asked as he cleaned a gash in Cnes's shoulder. 'There are hundreds of these birds. How will we ever kill them all?'

'Perhaps we could catch them?' said Ernamis.

'How?' Cnes asked.

'Well, a flock of birds that flies together lives together,' she said. 'Maybe we shouldn't meet them in the air, where they are strongest, but at the cliffs.'

Cnes was intrigued but uncertain. However, Échna could see where her sister was going. 'We'll use nets! In the Western Isles, on rare occasions when the seas withhold their catch of food, some fishing families send up their nets to catch birds.'

'Sounds delicious ... for a cat,' said Iollan.

'I know — I'd never swap a smoked mackerel for a smoked seagull,' Échna said, 'but it works, and those families never go hungry.'

Word was sent to the local fishing communities further down the coast, and within a few weeks a huge net threaded with the toughest of line was delivered. With care and quiet, the Fianna reached the Cliffs of Choitín and located the sidhe. Then, under cover of darkness, they lowered the sides of the net over the entrance to the sidhe — and waited. At daybreak, the demonic birds flew out to do more damage. However, as they did, they were caught in the net. The more they fought to free themselves the more they became entangled. And then, when every bird had been snared in the net, now heavy with their weight, the Fianna let it go. Down, down, down it dropped, smashing off the rocks and disappearing into the crashing waves below.

Not all monsters of the sidhe were in animal form. In the west, Cana led Cailte and Sárait against two ghostly sisters, Slat and Mumain. Both took malicious pleasure in enchanting and kidnapping young boys and girls. In the area of wet wilderness known as Connemara, many, many young children had disappeared in the past year. The two women with shorn hair and bright green cloaks would steal into hamlets and villages around dusk. They would find children who had not heeded the call to come home for supper and lead them into a sidhe that no one could discover. Bé Binn, a local queen of Connacht, recounted the tale of her son's disappearance to Cana. Her last sight of her little boy, deaf to her calls, was as he walked behind two women far in the distance under the evening gloom. Despite every effort, she and her men were unable to find the sidhe entrance.

But Cana had a plan that involved Cailte, who had three notable qualities. He was a great swordsman, a gifted musician and, though little older than Fionn, had the face of a child half his age. He was the perfect bait for Slat and Mumain. So, one evening, as he hurled alone on the outskirts of the village of Leitir Fraic, while Cana and Sárait lay in wait, the sisters approached.

As soon as they touched Cailte's hand he became enchanted. He dropped his hurl and walked after them, with Cana and Sárait in hot pursuit. But despite their best efforts, Cailte and his captors disappeared at the foot of a great cliff face. For some time, Cana and Sárait waited, unable to locate the sidhe entrance and growing concerned for Cailte. But then they heard it — the faint notes of a flute, a flute that had been hidden beneath Cailte's cloak, along with a knife, ready for when the enchantment wore off. The notes led them to an almost imperceptible path up the cliff face and to the sidhe entrance. When they went in, they found Cailte standing over the slain ghostly bodies of Slat and Mumain. That night, a hundred and fifty boys and girls came out of the sidhe to be reunited with their parents. One of them was the much-loved son of Bé Binn.

Many great tales came from those months, though it was Fionn's hunt for the Piast of Loch Cuan that was best remembered.

As Fionn, Donn and Lugach neared the great loch, they were met by the servants of Cruinn, the Chief of Loch Cuan, who invited them to stay the night as his guests. Over supper, he welcomed the support of the Fianna, something that had been absent for far too long.

'I am sorry that you and your people have been forgotten, but tomorrow we will begin our hunt for this monster,' said Fionn.

'I am glad of your help,' said Cruinn, 'but it will not be an easy feat.' He turned to his left and ushered forward a young man with dark, sombre eyes. 'This is

Daithí. He led our warring party against the Piast when it first emerged.' Cruinn addressed him. 'Go on, tell them what took place.'

Although he seemed reluctant at first, Daithí began to explain the events of that day. 'We had travelled out into the water, spears ready to kill the dreaded serpent. But, brave as I am, when I saw this Piast approach my blood ran cold. I looked into the darkness of its eyes and saw death. It had tusks of the ugliest shape, wider than the gates of Tara. It barely raised its whole head from the water, but we could see its back stretch out behind it like hills with a tail taller than an aspen tree! We threw our spears and struck with all our might as it reached us but to no avail. Its skin had scales as hard as rock. The spears barely scratched it. The only weakness that we saw was at the very front of its neck, where an arrow had lodged. There the flesh looked soft and more vulnerable. But the serpent kept it well protected. It was impossible to strike. Only after it crushed our boat did it raise its neck and plunge down on us as we floundered in the water.'

'How many of you were killed?' Fionn asked.

'All but me and two others. Many of our finest brothers and sisters were swallowed whole, never to be seen again!'

For many weeks Fionn and his warriors circled the lake, wary of straying out on a boat lest they suffer the same fate as Daithí and his force. However, it was to no avail. On the rare occasions they saw the Piast it was far from shore.

Early one winter's morning, Fionn stood sucking his thumb by a small brackish stream on the edge of the chief's home. Daithí joined him.

'Was the beast as big as you said?' Fionn asked.

'Yes, I'm afraid so.'

'And your fellow warriors swallowed whole?'

'Swallowed whole and brought down into the depths.'

As they spoke, their gaze was drawn to a little fish swimming in the reeds.

'A perch?' Fionn asked.

Just as Daithí opened his mouth to answer, a large marble-coloured pike emerged from below and gobbled the little thing whole. But just as it was about to disappear back down, it stopped and seemed to cough. Out popped the fish, alive and unharmed, and the pike turned and swam away.

'Well, I'll be,' said Daithí. 'It's a stickleback.'

'I have an idea!' Fionn announced excitedly, sitting down between Donn and Lugach. As he spoke he pulled out his magical treasure bag, an enchanted satchel created by Manannán Mac Lir, once leader of the Tuatha Dé Danann and a god of the sea. He had made it to help keep a hero of men and women safe from the threat of an evil Tuatha. One only had to put their hand in to obtain an item that would assist them in times of trouble.

'Brilliant,' said Donn. 'What have you in mind? A giant barbed spear? A harpoon maybe?'

Fionn placed some long daggers in front of his two fellow warriors before saying, 'I just need these and —' he put his hand in the treasure bag '— these!'

Donn stared at the needle and thread that Fionn had extracted. 'Could you not find something a little more ... magical in that bag? I mean, what are you going to do? Stitch the Piast's mouth shut?'

Fionn smiled as he described the stickleback he had seen and how, when the fish was swallowed whole by the pike, it had extended the sharp spines along its dorsal fin. 'This caused it to catch in the pike's gullet and be spat out. With your help, I will do the same.'

'How?' Donn asked.

'Both you and Lugach are from the clans that are known for travelling all over this island, fixing, mending, making and creating. You are masters with your hands. I want you to stitch these daggers into my tunic. When I brace my shoulders, I will draw them out. Once caught in the Piast's throat, I will go for its jugular and cut myself out where its neck is softest.'

'By the gods, Fionn!' said Lugach. 'Even for a dragon-slayer, that's a bit of a stretch.'

'Well, would you rather we take our chances on a boat together instead?'

The next day, Fionn sat on his own in a boat a little way out in the water. A shout from shore alerted him that he wasn't going to have to wait long. The Piast had not turned down the opportunity of a meal and was fast approaching from the north. As Daithí had mentioned, its head stayed low in the water, leaving only the rock-hard scales visible above. Then, less than fifty yards away from Fionn, it disappeared, and the lake fell eerily silent.

CRASH!

Without warning Fionn was thrown into the air. The Piast had broken through the hull of his boat, smashing it to smithereens. Fionn plunged into the icy-cold water and immediately knew he had a problem. He had over-looked the weight of the daggers. They were pulling him down. What to do? Be dragged below to drown or take the heavy shirt off and make himself an easy lunch? Moments later, the serpent made the decision for him and a ravenous mouth engulfed him.

On the shore, the onlookers' hearts sank. They had watched their hero first struggle, then disappear. But before the cold dread of loss could take hold of them, the Piast broke the surface, thrashing and flailing. For what seemed like an age, this writhing continued. Finally, it gave a death-cry and Fionn, victorious, cut his way through its throat where his stickleback tunic had held him.

Fionn's group was the last of the five bands of Fianna to arrive home, and by that time winter had firmly set in. He and his warriors were exhausted. And those who had returned from around the country were similarly so. Yes, they had rid the land of the monsters of the sidhe. And in doing so, they had gone a long way towards restoring the trust of their people. But Fionn knew it would take a while for his warriors to fully recover, and he could only hope that the wild, wintry seas would ensure that Goll would not come anytime soon. In the meantime, Art sent runners out with the Dord Fiann to call for new recruits.

A full moon later, the first flowers of spring were beginning to bloom. Fionn was talking to the High King in the Royal Hall when Cana entered.

'What news?' Fionn asked his dear friend.

'First, to tell you that shortly after dawn we welcomed the arrival of some new would-be warriors. People are answering our call. It seems trust has been restored. Chieftains around the country want to show their faith by sending us their young men and women to join the Fianna.'

'That's great,' said Fionn. Then, seeing a twinkle in Cana's eye, he asked, 'What else?'

'I know you like riddles, so try this one. I have four legs but am not a table. I have a bark but am not a tree. I like to run but am not water. What am I?'

'Easy,' Fionn replied. 'A dog.'

'Yes, but what type of dog?' Cana smiled.

'Huh? I don't know.'

'I'll give you a clue. It's currently eating your breakfast.'

Fionn left the High King and ran out to where the Fianna often had their meals. There, tucking into the breakfast Fionn had left to cool, was the largest puppy he had ever seen. 'What is this?'

'This is Conbec,' Cana answered. 'It's a wolfhound pup, a gift from the Chief of Loch Cuan.'

# THE HOUNDS AND HORSES

SMASH!

    'Get out of here!'

    CLATTER!

  'Out! Out! Out!'

  CRASH!

'Fionn!'

The roars of Chief Druid Caicer rang out from his chambers. Bounding from his room was a dog – all legs and shaggy mane. Though it was still only a pup it had already grown to a warrior's hip height. As it sprang away, its rump swung clumsily against a table, knocking it and everything it held across the hall.

  CLASH!

49

A short time later, Fionn sheepishly poked his head around the door of Caicer's study. 'Er, Chief Druid? I heard you were looking for me?'

'You heard?' Caicer said. 'Well, if you heard I was looking for you, I'm surprised you didn't hear the commotion caused before that. Your pup, Fionn, is becoming more and more disruptive each and every day.'

'You mean little Conbec?' Fionn asked innocently.

Fionn knew very well that the puppy he had received from the Chief of Loch Cuan was no longer little. For the first few months, he would allow Conbec into his own bed. This stopped when Conbec grew so large that, come morning, Fionn had been finding himself kicked out and lying on the floor!

'Of course I'm talking about Conbec!' Caicer continued crossly. 'He might have been cute when he arrived, but he is now a very, very big pup and is causing too much trouble. Pooing in the royal banqueting hall is one thing but destroying my study as he looks for an old bone or knocking over a half-dozen market stalls, sending food into the air and onto the ground, is another. It's bad enough that he will eat enough food to feed a family if you let him, but he is now scaring the cooks in the kitchen and the servants throughout the royal palace.'

'He's just a big softie.' Even this got a sharp look from Caicer.

'He *can* be a big softie, but he snapped at Ossnat yesterday when she refused to hand over a leg of meat.'

'He wouldn't bite!' Fionn said, surprised even by the thought of it.

'Fionn, he is a wolfhound. He is supposed to bite — just not his friends!'

Caicer looked at Fionn, whose head was now lowered. Fionn had turned sixteen over the summer, and while he had one foot in adulthood, a large part of his heart was still very young. Caicer knew he couldn't be too hard on a boy and his dog. 'Look, Fionn. The old poems are clear. They state that the wolfhound is our friend and that a strong Fianna force should have hounds at its core. However, there are reasons they have not been used for generations. They are hard to train and can be more trouble than they are worth. I want you to pay a visit to the warrior Connla. He has been with the Fianna for a long time now and has a way with dogs. He should be able to help.'

That afternoon, Fionn went looking for Connla.

'Hello, anyone here?' Fionn called as he arrived at the group of huts where many of the warriors were stationed. 'Connla?'

'Hi, Fionn,' Diorraing answered, coming out from a nearby hut. 'You looking for Connla?'

'Yes, the Chief Druid suggested I have a word with him about training Conbec.'

'Ah yes, I've heard he has been getting up to some mischief,' Diorraing said as he gently scratched the base of Conbec's ears, much to the hound's satisfaction.

'You seem to know what you're doing. Any advice?'

'Not really.' He grinned. 'We always had animals around when I was growing up. I'm used to them but, to be honest, I'm more of a cat person. Now, if you want to know everything about dogs' — he nodded over Fionn's shoulder — 'then here's your man.'

'So, you came to see a man about a dog,' Connla said, sitting down, his freckled face giving his forty years a more youthful appearance.

'Yes, the Chief Druid said you can train wolfhounds. Is it true?'

'Yes, it is. Our clan has had hounds for as far back as can be remembered. The dogs are like members of our family.'

'I want to bring them back into the Fianna, and I plan to ask every clan in the country that has wolfhounds to send one to Tara, just as was done in the oldest of times. But there's no point bringing wolfhounds into the Fianna if I can't even train this pup.'

Conbec, sensing he was being spoken about, slipped away and climbed up onto the wide windowsill.

'Down!' barked Connla. He stood up from the table and led Conbec off the sill and over to a corner of the room, where he laid down a blanket for Conbec to snooze on. He then returned to sit beside Fionn. 'If you have come to ask for my help to train Conbec – and every dog you are sent – then the answer is yes. It would be my honour. But it's important to remember that, while I can help train the hounds, you must become their leader.'

'What do you mean?'

'Well, all dogs are pack animals. Like humans, they crave the company of others. They're not like Diorraing's cats, who are often happiest alone and would walk over your dead body for a sup of milk.'

'I'd step over your dead body for a sup of milk!' Diorraing shot back, laughing.

'As pack animals,' Connla went on, 'dogs need a leader to provide guidance and direction. If a dog doesn't have a leader it takes on that role itself. And that's when the trouble starts. It's why they bite unexpectedly, bark through the night, don't listen to commands and smash all the Chief Druid's cups and plates. If you want to train wolfhounds and then command them, you need to be the pack leader.'

Fionn nodded. 'How do I do that? I'm hardly expected to wrestle for it, am I?'

'Would you like to wrestle a grown wolfhound the size of a deer with teeth as long as your finger? No, you don't wrestle. It's a lot easier than that. You just need to follow a few simple rules.'

'Like what?'

Connla held his hand up in front of him and began using his thumb and fingers to count. 'First, never let a dog take a position above you. You are the top dog and you need to show that clearly in every setting. Second, never feed your dog before yourself, even if you arrive home stuffed full after a king's feast. Make sure your hound sees you eat something, no matter how small, even if it is just a few hazelnuts, before you feed them. Third, never greet them immediately when you return from being away, no matter how excited they may appear. Only when they have settled can you shower them with affection.'

'That all seems very harsh.' Fionn said.

'It does, doesn't it? But it is a long way from wrestling them, and I swear you will never see a happier hound than one that has a leader it can rely on.'

In the space of three or four weeks, Connla's tips and training began to show results. Conbec listened more. He became happier, more settled, less chaotic, and there were far fewer complaints about his behaviour. By late autumn, Conbec was bigger again and fully trained. Fionn knew then it was time to put a call out for more wolfhounds.

Soon, wolfhound pups and much older dogs arrived from all across the country. And throughout the winter, Connla schooled them.

That same winter, across the water, Goll made camp in the valleys of Cymru, a land that one day would become known as Wales. It was his third winter away from Ireland, and he had made slow but steady progress in creating a force strong enough to lead back to Ireland. He had developed alliances with local kings and chiefs across the land and beyond — with some by using the gold and silver he'd plundered from Tara as he fled, with others through the promise of later reward. It was one of those, Benne, whom he was speaking to one bitterly cold night in that third winter.

'Sit,' Goll said, indicating the long tree trunk in front of the campfire, the only source of comfort in the sleety rain.

'Welcome back to these parts,' Benne replied as he took his seat. Though he smiled often, there was no joy in his face. This joylessness was reinforced by the square ridge of his nose, which showed that it had been broken many times. He was as big as Goll, with shoulders just as solid. But unlike Goll, who was bald and beardless, Benne had a long mane of tangled brown hair and a great growth of facial hair to go with it. Neither man was someone you would want to meet on a dark night – or a bright day, for that matter. 'So, what news?'

'Word from Ireland,' Goll began, 'is that the Fianna are training dogs once more.'

'Dogs? What for?' Benne laughed. 'To play fetch with?'

'These aren't just any dogs – they are fierce.'

'How fierce?'

'They call them wolfhounds because they can hunt wolves, so pretty fierce. Once trained, they're worth two soldiers on the battlefield. I want two of them – two pups, one male, one female. We'll breed them together and with our other dogs. And soon we'll have our own pack to bring back with us.'

'And you want me and my ship to go get these dogs?' Benne asked.

'Yes and you will be well rewarded.' With that, a warrior standing next to Goll threw a small pouch to Benne. 'Half now, half when you have them.'

'It will take some time. I will need to find someone who understands dogs to help me steal them.'

'I will be back again by midsummer. Have the hounds ready by then.'

As Benne and his men left Goll's camp, the warrior next to Goll spoke. 'Next summer, brother? We're going to breed hounds? For a year? Two? How long must we stay in this miserable land? We should leave now and attack. We have more than a dozen chiefs and rulers who will fight with us, several hundred men, and many great warriors who are equal to those of the Fianna. Why wait?'

Goll looked at his younger brother, Conan. 'Because it is not enough. You've heard the reports coming to us from Ireland. The Fianna have grown stronger. Chiefs and clans from across the island are repledging support and are ready to supply them with soldiers if called upon. To get our revenge, we must win, and we still don't have enough forces.'

'Maybe I can help?'

Both men were immediately on their feet, swords drawn, looking past the fire at the figure who had just spoken.

'Who are you? How did you get past our men?' Goll said.

The figure didn't answer but instead stepped around the flames before taking down his hood. 'Have you no warmer greeting for your old Chief Druid?'

It had been many years since they had last met, but the druid had changed little. His eyes were as serpent-like as before, and he was still hunched. Only his beard, which was now longer and greyer, showed that years had passed.

'What brings you here, Chief Druid?'

'I am no longer Chief Druid. And what brings me here is the same thing that brings you. I want to return to Ireland and take back what was mine. And I can help you be much more than champion of the Fianna. I can make you king.'

'What makes you think we need your help?' said Conan.

'Because, as your older brother has already said, you don't have enough men. But I can get you another army.'

'How?' Goll asked.

'The Dealra Dubh will provide one.'

'Go on,' said Goll.

'When Conn banished me, he forced me to leave behind my staff, as well as the Great Book of Moytura, a sacred text that helped me communicate with the Dealra Dubh. If you help me get these back, I will once again have the strength to call on the Dealra Dubh. I have found the entrance to where he resides. Once opened, you will soon have another army. Together with forces from abroad, no Fianna will stand in our way.'

'And for this, what do you or the Dealra Dubh want?'

'My position as Chief Druid again and devotion to the Dealra Dubh, a small price to pay to make you king.'

'I don't know,' Conan said, looking worried. 'Do we need this dark magic?'

Goll spoke. 'You said it yourself, brother — how long must we stay in this miserable land?'

Back in Tara, not only wolfhounds had arrived over the winter. More recruits had also found their way to the royal capital. Of those who came, two in particular would have a profound impact. The first was a nameless young man, slight but athletic with a shock of red hair. The boy appeared to be mute, unable to speak a single word. But he could hear perfectly well and was a natural with animals, particularly dogs. He soon found a place helping Connla, who gave him the name Covey, 'the hound of Meath'. Covey learned quickly and was a great listener. Occasionally, it seemed that a cloud hung over him, and Connla would sometimes catch him early in the morning, looking forlornly to the rising sun.

As the days lengthened, Fionn and many of his fellow warriors began to take the growing number of hounds out on hunting forays to test them. During one of these hunts, Fionn and some fellow warriors had been out with Conbec and two new hounds, Steallaire and Fuaim. The youthful enthusiasm of the hounds had driven a family of wild boar into the Fianna, causing more than a few cuts and bruises. Fionn received a nasty cut along his heel.

Usually Eitne treated such injuries. But she was away, and it fell to a young woman by the name of Sadb to treat Fionn's wounds. She was the second arrival who would have a far-reaching impact.

'Ow! What's that?' Fionn said, as a cold honey-coloured paste was applied to the wound.

'It's a mixture of witch hazel and yarrow, and yes, before you ask, it's meant to sting. That's how we know it's working.'

Fionn looked up at the girl who was treating him. She was roughly his age, perhaps a little older, with fair hair nearly as bright as his but longer. Her almost translucent grey eyes caught him staring at her and he felt his cheeks redden. 'I don't know you,' he said.

'No, you don't. I am not a Fianna warrior. I just heal Fianna warriors. My name is Sadb.'

'You know, Eitne Ollamda can handle a sword as well as anyone.'

'I heard. I don't handle any weapons, if you're wondering. In fact, I think violence is pretty pointless and only begets more violence.'

'Ow!' Fionn yelled again. 'Are you sure about that?'

'I responded to the call this winter because I heard that these Fianna were different — that they wanted to help and protect people. I came to offer my skills in healing.'

'Where did you learn how to heal?'

'I'm not sure. I never knew my father, and my mother died when I was very little, so it was my aunt who looked after me. I spent many hours in the nearby forest. Its flora and fauna were a language that came naturally to me, and I learned everything about the plants, flowers and herbs that grew there. That's it.'

'That's it?' Fionn said.

'Yes, that's it — I'm finished with your heel.'

'Oh yes, sorry. Er ...' Fionn hesitated. 'I was wondering if you might like to meet up later. We caught that boar in the end and are feasting later.'

'I don't really eat meat,' Sadb replied. 'The forest offers enough other food so I don't need to, but I'll see you tomorrow.' She smiled.

'Yeah?'

'Yes, when you come here so I can change that bandage.'

The next morning, and on the days that followed, Sadb changed Fionn's bandage. And though each treatment brought with it the pain of her cleansing lotion, her company more than made up for it. When his heel finally healed, his visits continued. Fionn soon found the beginning of what would prove to be love, and the two would become inseparable whenever Fionn was home in Tara and not strengthening the defences and forts around the island.

By late spring, Connla and Covey had succeeded in preparing a large pack of wolfhounds for battle. One morning, Fionn departed with a large group of warriors and hounds for a hunt off to the hillier north-west. As they left, Covey appeared even more preoccupied than normal.

'Is it the approaching full moon that's distracting you today?' Connla asked playfully, trying to cheer him up. 'Are you more wolf than hound?'

Covey smiled apologetically before beginning his daily chores.

At this time, Connla was treating a sick young wolf-hound called Feargach. A few days previously, having gone astray from a hunting party led by Sárait and Cál in Ulster, it had fallen into a crevice. It had taken quite some time and thought but they had managed to finally fish it out from below. When they did, while it had survived the fall relatively unscathed, it was covered in small bites.

'Bats,' Connla had thought when Sárait and Cál brought the hound to him to treat. After a few days the bites seemed to heal. However, Feargach's overall health only grew worse. The hound became ill, went off his food and lacked all energy.

Connla now looked at him. Despite his best efforts, the poor dog looked terrible. His mouth would not close, causing foam to form around his jaws.

'There, there, Feargach,' Connla whispered to the hound, who stared blankly into space in the pen where he was being kept. 'Let me try some medicine I got Eitne to make up yesterday.' As Connla turned towards the door, a spark appeared in Feargach's eyes and without warning he shot up, bared his teeth and rushed at Connla, who was oblivious to this peril.

'Look out!' screamed Covey, alerting Connla, who had just enough time to duck out of the way of Feargach's lethal pounce. Feargach landed, tumbled and turned to attack again. However, Covey was instantly inside the pen, axe in hand, and slew the hound and whatever it was that had possessed him.

'You spoke,' Connla said as he picked himself up off the ground. 'You can speak?'

Covey slowly turned round. 'I'm sorry,' he replied. It was a thick accent that Connla couldn't place.

'Sorry? Why should you be sorry? You saved my life.' But as he spoke, Connla could see Covey's knuckles whiten as his grip on the axe tightened. 'Covey. Covey? Whatever it is that you – *No!*'

SMACK.

A rivulet of blood from Connla's head dripped onto the ground. His young assistant quickly put two little pups – one male, one female – into a large cloth sack and swiftly departed.

'How is he?' Fionn asked.

'He has a bad headache and his pride is hurt, but he'll be okay,' Eitne replied as she, Fionn, the High King and Cana entered the Chief Druid's rooms, where Connla now lay.

Fionn and his band of warriors had returned from the hunt in the late afternoon to hear that Connla had been left for dead. His assistant, Covey, had disappeared and a couple of young pups were missing.

'Are you all right?' Fionn asked as he reached Connla's side.

'I'll be fine.'

'What happened?'

'I don't know. Covey seemed a little more distant than normal this morning, but I thought little of it. We began our work. I was in with Feargach and ...'

'He attacked you.'

'Yes, he did, although he wasn't my Feargach any more. Something had turned in the dog. It had been bitten by a bat, and the bite had changed it. You could see it in his eyes. I should have known not to turn my back on him, but Covey saved me.'

'Saved you?' said Cana. 'And then he nearly killed you?'

'No, he knew what he was doing. He could have taken my head off with that axe, but he didn't.'

'You said he spoke?' Fionn said.

'Yes, he did, but his accent was unlike anything I have ever heard.'

'What did it sound like?'

'It's hard to describe and he only spoke a few words, but when he said "sorry" his "r" was guttural.'

'From across the sea?' said Art.

'It would explain why he pretended to be mute,' said Cana. 'He would have been noticed immediately. Maybe he was always going to take the puppies — it was just bad timing that Feargach attacked when he did. After speaking, he had no choice but to take them there and then.'

While Cana was talking, Ossnat arrived.

'Any news?' Fionn asked.

'Yes. I picked up his tracks in the mud a mile north of here. A solitary walker with deep footprints, which suggested he was carrying a load.'

'The pups?'

'I expect so, and what little of his things he had. His hut is completely empty. He seems to have turned east before he got to the Boyne.'

'I'm guessing he was afraid of coming across some of our soldiers at the river's mouth,' Fionn said, 'and that he is going straight for the coast, where the month's high tide might help bring a boat further ashore to collect him. Right, Cana, gather a half-dozen warriors!'

As they turned to leave, Connla spoke. 'There is a rag in my hut that Covey was using. His smell should be all over it. Take the hounds Saothar, Luas and Boladh, and give them the rag. Their sense of smell far exceeds our own. With Covey's scent in their noses, they will track him down. I guarantee it.'

A few minutes later, a small band of warriors, led by Fionn and Ossnat and directed by the three hounds, was heading east, following the trail Ossnat had found. Just as Connla predicted, the dogs soon took off in determined pursuit. However, while Covey was laden down by two sizeable wolfhound pups, he had a few hours' head start, which proved invaluable. When the band arrived at the long, flat, sandy shores of An Inse, it was too late. In the distance was the unmistakable sight of a boat sailing away.

The next morning, under the watchful eye of the High King, Fionn led a conversation among the Fianna to decide their next course of action.

'We should leave immediately and take back what is ours!'

'And risk how many men and women for two pups?'

'Those pups are our pups, and they are loyal to us.'

'We can't just let them be taken.'

'What does that tell our enemies?'

'That you can come and pillage us with ease?'

'Our enemies are coming. We can't afford to be away at sea when they arrive.'

The arguments went back and forth. Fionn listened carefully to all before passing his judgement. 'There is worth in everything that has been said, but we need to choose just one path,' he began. 'It is a risk. You are right when you say this, Lugach. However, Ernamis is also right when she says that these are our hounds. They were gifted to us from the clans around this country to help us protect them. They were not gifted so that others could breed them and use them against us, and that is what I fear will happen. Only Ireland has wolfhounds, and this is one edge I do not want to give our neighbours. And yes, Eitne, if we leave, then what happens if we are attacked? The answer is I don't know, but I do know that if we don't take back what is ours, then, as Cnes has said, other foreign groups will see this as a licence to come and plunder at will.' Fionn then turned to address the High King directly. 'I propose that a band of us goes and takes back the two pups.'

Art sat back in his chair. To his left sat the old High King, Conn. Up until now, the decisions that Art or Fionn had made had seemed relatively straightforward. But this was a bigger decision, weighed down with more risk. And Art, not his father, had to choose wisely. 'Fionn, I trust your judgement and I give you my blessing to take back the pups. However, I ask you to trust others in your command to lead this raid so that you remain at home and continue to prepare for war, which I believe is drawing ever closer.'

That evening Fionn thought about what Art had said. The next day, seeing the wisdom in the king's judgement, he appointed Cana in his stead. Going with her would be Ernamis, whose seafaring skills would help navigate them over, and Ossnat, whose tracking skills would be vital. Diorraing and Sárait would also go, with the hounds Saothar, Luas and Boladh in tow. Meanwhile, Fionn would send Iollan and a band of warriors north and Cnes and another group south to instruct and help clans to make ready their coastal defences. After a fortnight of preparations, all were ready, with Cana's group setting sail for Cymru.

The seas were kind, with a strong westerly gale. After a day and night of travel, they arrived just before dawn, mooring safely in an isolated cove. Over the next few weeks they slowly progressed. Always under cover of darkness, they probed and prodded the coastal areas, hoping that their hounds would pick up a scent. For a while it looked like they would be unsuccessful and that no trace would be found. However, as they were about to give up hope, Saothar's ears pricked as she caught a scent of something. It was Covey and the pups. The warriors began their journey inland. After two nights of careful trekking they came across an encampment of men. Though it was dark, the flames from their campfire shone brightly off their swords. These were warriors and well armed too. Cana and her company would have to be careful.

Sárait looked out through the darkness. 'Ssshh,' she whispered to Cana and Ernamis, 'someone's coming.' She tightened her grip on the hilt of her sword before relaxing again. 'It's okay — it's Diorraing and Ossnat.'

Returning from their noiseless recce of the camp, the warriors were not alone. Alongside them was the bloodied, bruised but unmistakable figure of Covey.

'What did you bring him back for?' Sárait muttered angrily. 'You should have slit his throat and left him with his friends!'

'Well, it turns out that they're not very good friends,' Ossnat said. 'We found him bound and imprisoned at the edge of their camp. This blood and bruising is not from our hand but from those around that fire. We counted maybe twenty armed men.'

'And the pups?' Cana asked.

'In a cage close to them. It will be impossible to free the pups without a fight.'

Cana looked at Covey with cold disdain. 'We know you can talk, so explain yourself. Tell us why we shouldn't leave you for dead on the ground — like you did to Connla?'

'How is he?' Covey asked hoarsely.

'Alive, no thanks to you. Now, continue.'

'My name is Artúir, and my two brothers and I were sheep herders on the foothills of the Lodán Mountains, not far from here. We lived simple and happy lives. A few moons ago, a group of bandits from the flat plains below arrived at our hamlet one dark winter's evening. They were led by a villain of the name Benne. He is sitting at that very campfire right now. He made it clear that he knew our skill with dogs and that one of us was needed to use these skills to help him get something very important. If we didn't help, then every sheep and ram that we had would be taken away and all they would leave behind would be our heads. I volunteered, to keep my brothers, my family and my flock alive, but in the end it didn't matter. Benne did not keep his word, and my family were dead when I came back, our flock slaughtered and sold. I didn't want to hurt Connla. I had planned to take the pups the very day he discovered my lie. A ship was meeting me on that full moon.'

'Why does Benne want the pups?' Cana asked.

'He doesn't. They're not for him but for one of your countrymen. I overheard him talk of the gold and silver he is soon due from a one-eyed Irishman.'

'Goll,' Cana said.

'Yes, Goll. I've heard that name mentioned. He and his warriors are expected soon to take the hounds.'

'Could we wait for Goll and kill him when he arrives?' Sárait asked.

'You won't kill him,' Covey said. 'They say he has a retinue of some fifty battle-hardened warriors who travel with him, and twenty of Benne's force have already left to welcome them. That's seventy enemies you'd have to face.'

'Well, I don't mind sharing,' Sárait said scornfully.

'He's right,' said Cana. 'Maybe if we got close enough and had a clean shot we could kill him, but we would all surely die in the process. And while I know, Sárait, you fear death probably as much as you fear sleep, Fionn didn't ask me to lead you all to your doom and I am not about to start. So there are twenty men left in the camp, then?'

'By my count, yes,' said Ossnat. 'That's still a big number.'

Cana smiled. 'With three hounds, the element of surprise and five warriors, I fancy our chances.'

'Allow me to join you then,' Covey asked, 'and that'll make six of us.'

The skirmish that followed was swift, bloody and effective. Benne and his force were crushed in a matter of minutes, with two puppies freed and a young shepherd avenged.

As the Fianna nursed their wounds, Ossnat made a startling discovery — a horse bigger than any she had ever seen in Ireland was tethered to a tree at the edge of the camp. 'What sort of horse is this?' she asked.

'This is what we call a horse here,' Covey answered. 'What you have in Ireland are what we'd call ponies.'

'Ponies?'

'Yes, ponies. This here is a horse. They are also very, very fast. Watch.' Covey quickly hopped up onto it, loosened the rope it was bound by and set off into the distance.

'Did he just escape?' Diorraing asked. 'Because if he did, I think we'd better get out of here.' Thankfully, though, Covey reappeared at speed from another direction, bringing the horse to a sharp halt in front of the warriors.

'Wow!' said Cana. 'Right, Diorraing, take the pups, and let's take the horse too.'

'I've got a better idea if you'll listen and allow me to make up for my betrayal,' Covey said.

He told them of a herd of horses some dozen miles to the south that belonged to a chief who had allied himself with Goll. 'Give me a chance to prove myself and I will bring you this herd.'

It was a risk, but one Cana thought was worth taking. 'If we are not back at the boat by daybreak, leave without us,' she told Ernamis before joining Covey in the saddle of Benne's horse and riding off. Two hours later they had arrived.

'What now?' Cana asked.

'Step down, open the paddock gate and watch. Trust me.'

What Cana saw next was nothing short of remarkable. Instead of making any attempt to corral the horses, Covey rode directly at them, scattering them this way and that. Cana was full sure that someone from the nearby camp would hear and sound the alarm. But they didn't. Covey then turned and galloped at the horses a second time, and then a third, before returning to the gate and a shocked Cana, to whom he said, 'Quick, jump up, we're going!'

'But what of the horses?'

'Watch and see!'

And with that, Cana turned round to see the most extraordinary sight she could imagine. Every one of the horses was beginning to walk in single file behind them. 'What's happening? Is this some sort of magic?'

'No. As well as being fast, horses are also playful — and very, very nosey. When I galloped at them, they scattered, but they loved the fun and excitement of it. And now that we are leaving, their game has ended, and they want to play more. They want me to continue chasing them. But I won't. Instead, we'll lead them all the way to the beach.'

Cana watched the line of some thirty horses trotting behind them.

Covey smiled. 'You're gonna need a bigger boat.'

He was right. But with the gold and silver they had taken from Benne and his men, they were able to swap their boat for a larger one in a coastal fishing village.

With kind winds and a calm sea, they reached Irish shores a few days later — less than a month after they had left. That they all arrived back safe, and with not just the two pups but a team of horses too, was a source of great joy, and Cailte even composed a poem in their honour. Fionn spoke at length to Covey and accepted him into what became Covey's new family. And that night a great feast was held in Tara. But if Fionn hoped to have a nice sleep the next day, he was sorely mistaken. An hour before dawn, a loud banging could be heard coming from the great door of the palace. It was Cál, who had accompanied Iollan in the north.

'What is it?' Fionn asked groggily as he entered the hall, where Cál now stood.

'I'm afraid it's not good,' Cál announced to Fionn and the Fianna warriors, who had now all awoken from their slumber and were trailing into the hall behind Fionn. 'I've been travelling since yesterday and all through the night. A giant has arrived on our shores and is threatening to lay waste to everything in his path.'

'A giant?' Fionn repeated. 'Has he come for the horses?'

'The horses?' Cál replied. 'No, Fionn — he has come for you.'

# THE GIANT'S CAUSEWAY

'Tell me again,' Fionn said. 'A giant has arrived on our northern shores. What sort of giant?'

'A big one,' Cál replied.

'Yes, but how big? The size of Diorraing here?'

'Bigger.'

'By how much?'

'Three, maybe four —'

'Inches?' Fionn asked.

'No.'

'Feet?'

'No. Times. The giant is maybe three or four times his size.'

Cál explained to the royal court of Tara that,

alongside Iollan, he had watched this colossus anchor a great boat off the north Antrim coast. And then he swam to and climbed up the hexagonal coastal steps that were said to have once formed a causeway between Ireland and Scotland. The speed and dexterity with which he rose from the sea were as astonishing as his vast size.

'We could see that he was shaped like any of us, but everything about him was super-sized, from head to toe. His muscles were rippling beneath his tunic. His dark hair, moustache and beard, still dripping with seawater, were like overgrown bushes filled with briars. His appearance was fearsome, as were the hand-axe, knife and huge sword that dangled from his waist. If the giant was coming in peace, he certainly was not dressed for it. Iollan knew that confronting him would have visited death on many of us, so he took a different tack.'

'Hello,' Iollan had announced, 'what gives us the pleasure of welcoming you to our shores?'

'My name is Benandonner, and I need no welcome. What I want is Fionn Mac Cumhaill!'

Benandonner's gaze was misty, as if he was there but wasn't at the same time.

'Oh, I know him well. Can I ask what you want from Fionn?'

'I want to take his head.'

'Right.' Iollan gulped. 'I'm sure Fionn's body will be disappointed to hear that, but unfortunately for you he isn't here now. Any chance you could call back another time?'

'No,' Benandonner replied sternly. 'I will wait, and while I do I will destroy a village each and every day he delays me.'

'We wouldn't be wanting that,' Iollan answered, trying to keep calm and stop his voice from breaking. 'Well, I do know where we can find him, so maybe you could come with me, Benan ...?'

'... donner,' the giant growled.

'Yes, Benandonner, come with me. I am sure Fionn will be delighted to meet you.'

As they turned and started walking away from the coast, Iollan pulled Cál aside and instructed him to, as soon as the opportunity arose, sneak away from their convoy, travel to Tara and let Fionn know of the giant's presence. In the meantime, Iollan would take him on the slow road to Donegal.

After Cál concluded, Fionn turned to the Chief Druid. 'Have you ever heard of a man of such size?'

'It sounds like it could be one of the Maelán,' Caicer replied.

'Who are they?'

'They were once believed to be pure legend, a clan of man-eating giants that lived in a hidden glen on the Isle of Manau — a figment of a parent's imagination, spoken of only to scare children into doing as they were told. But then one day your granduncle, a man by the name of Ros, arrived at the court of King Fedlimid the Lawful, Conn's father. Ros had left these shores many years before to travel the known and unknown world. Upon his return, for weeks he entertained the royal court with tall tales. His last stop before he came back to Ireland was a small island not a hundred miles to our east, nestled in the sea between us, Scotland and Cymru.

'He claimed that in a hidden glen in the very centre of the island lived the Maelán, a race of giants. They were not an intelligent people but had immense strength and were lightning-fast for their size. He claimed they were each twenty feet tall and led by a colossus who was bigger again — by the name of Benandonner.'

'The same giant? But that must have been —'

'A long time ago. Yes, it was.' The old High King, Conn, who was sitting quietly in a dark corner of the royal court, as was his habit those days, spoke up.

'Why didn't they eat him?' Fionn asked.

'I asked the same question,' Conn answered. 'They didn't eat people, Ros said. We are too bony for them and they preferred to feast on boars and stags. Ros boasted that he could have stayed in their company for as long as he'd wanted. Although fierce in appearance, they were generally a peace-loving people, he claimed. But your granduncle was a greedy man, very different from your grandfather Trénmor. Ros became fixated on the large amethyst-studded golden finger rings the giants wore. They were as big as torc necklaces, and one night as they all slept, he stole away with one. Benandonner woke and gave chase. As the giant closed in on him, Ros was forced to drop the heavy ring and escape down a river, nearly drowning himself as he did.

'I was only a child then, but like everyone else, I laughed, believing this to be just another tall tale. But then Ros pulled out a button bigger than a plate and claimed that it had come from one of the giant's tunics.'

'Since then,' Caicer concluded, 'there have been occasional rumours of these giants, but no one has ever seen or heard of one ... until now.'

Fionn sat silently for some time, sucking his thumb, weighing his options.

'What are you thinking, Fionn?' Cana finally asked.

'I am thinking that Iollan was right not to confront the giant when it arrived, especially if it is as big as Cál describes. Although I'm not sure I have a choice, not if

I want to prevent it laying waste to northern villages, whose trust we've only recently won back.'

'But you also want to keep your head,' Sadb, who had been silent up until now but who was rarely far from Fionn, said, before adding wryly, 'because they don't grow back.'

Fionn smiled. 'Something just doesn't make sense. If Ros was right and these giants were peace-loving, why come over the sea to kill me? And don't tell me he's still sore about that button.'

Caicer spoke. 'Maybe some enchantment is behind his crossing to Ireland. Cál spoke of his dull and misty eyes.'

'Well, if the giant is under a spell, is there any way we can break it?' Fionn asked.

'Possibly,' the Chief Druid answered. 'It depends on how powerful the sorcery behind it is.'

'Maybe I can help,' said Eitne. 'I know of a potion that might work. If I can make it, and you add your magic words, it should be strong enough. It just depends on whether I can find the right herbs.'

'But what then?' Cana asked. 'If the giant is entranced and we break this spell, we will still be left with a thirty-foot colossus far from home. Peace-loving or not, that's not a great recipe.'

Fionn thought hard and then smiled. 'I might have a plan. But I will need Covey. Send word to get him.'

Fionn turned to Art. 'How many blacksmiths and cart-wrights live inside the walls of Tara?'

'A dozen, I believe, of each.'

'And what of cloth-makers?' Fionn asked, looking at Diorraing with a mischievous smile.

'Twice that number.'

'Well, with your permission, I'd like you to ask them to make something for me.'

'I'll have them woken at once,' said Art.

Just then, Covey arrived.

'You say your horses are stronger, faster and more powerful than the ones that we keep. Is that really true?' Fionn asked.

'It is,' Covey said, 'especially in the right hands.'

'And can they pull weight behind them if needed?'

'They can. Better than any oxen and much quicker.'

'Good, they may need to. I'm going to ask you to stay here with Eitne and Caicer and help them ready a mixture. In the meantime, myself, Cana, Diorraing, Lugach and Lachtna will travel to the Maghera Caves in Donegal with these horses. When the mixture is ready, take the quickest horses of those left and come after us. But there are a couple of other things I will need you to bring as well.'

A short time later, Fionn and his fellow warriors gathered, but someone was missing. 'There are only four of us. Where's Lachtna?'

'He says he is sick,' Lugach answered. 'Something he has eaten.'

'I'll take his place,' Ossnat said, happy to be back in the company of Diorraing.

'Fine. I'll talk with Lachtna when I return,' said Fionn. 'Right, let's go.'

As Covey had suggested, the group rode swiftly on these larger beasts, their wolfhounds accompanying them throughout. By the time Iollan and the giant made it to the Big Gap, a mountain pass that ran through that part of the country, Fionn and Lugach, both on horseback and having left the others, with Conbec at their side, were awaiting them. As the huge figure of Benandonner loomed Conbec began to growl. 'Steady, boy,' Fionn breathed, before greeting the approaching party.

'Iollan!' Fionn shouted as his fellow Fianna warrior came near. 'This is a surprise. And I see you have brought a guest. How wonderful!'

Benandonner grunted crossly. 'Who are you? And where is Fionn?'

'My name is ... Demne and this is Lugach — we are servants to Fionn. You must have just missed him — he passed here not ten minutes ago to go hunting. But don't worry, he shouldn't be too long. We've been expecting you. However, I wasn't told what it is you are here to see Fionn about?'

The giant growled. 'I am here to kill him and take his head.'

'Oh! That's a pity. I'm sure he will be sad to hear that. Why do you want his head?'

'I ... don't ... know.' Benandonner appeared momentarily flummoxed before lashing out, 'I just want his head!'

From the giant's response and his blank eyes, Fionn believed Caicer was right. The giant was under some mysterious control. The only question was whether Fionn could break that control without spilling blood.

'Well, my master has a feast prepared. Come, join us. After all, you can't be cutting off each other's heads on an empty stomach, can you?'

As Fionn led them westwards a heavy rain began to fall.

Iollan caught up with Lugach. 'Do you mind telling me what it is you are sitting on?'

'Oh, this? It's a horse, just a bigger version of the ones we're used to. Aren't they great? Cana found a load of them. Jump up there and take the weight off your feet.'

Iollan climbed up behind Lugach. 'Does Fionn have a plan for when we get to the caves?' Iollan asked, looking nervously back at the giant. 'Or are you planning on killing him with indigestion?'

'I guess it depends on what turns up on the menu,' Lugach answered.

'Wonderful, just wonderful!' Iollan replied sarcastically.

A few hours later, the rain had lessened to a drizzle and the strange procession of riders, dog and giant reached the Caves of Maghera, a collection of clefts along the coast of west Donegal. They arrived in the falling darkness to warmth and brightness from the fires that the rest of Fionn's band had lit.

Dipping under the cave entrance and into its shelter, they were met first by Cana.

'This must be Benandonner,' she said with a wide smile. 'I've heard you came to see Fionn?'

'He's come to cut off his head,' Iollan added.

'Really?' Cana said with surprise. 'That was my favourite part of him! You'll leave us the rest of him, though, won't you?'

Benandonner peered at this strange woman before looking around the cave, inspecting the figures of Eitne, Covey and Ossnat, who stood waiting for them.

'Oh, if you're wondering, Fionn has yet to return. I'm guessing he must have taken shelter in these wet conditions and will be back soon. But let's not delay. Here is our finest cook, Eitne Ollamda, who has prepared the most magnificent feast for you that our servants will now serve. Let's not allow it to go cold.'

While Cana continued to talk to the giant and Ossnat and Covey began bringing out food, Fionn caught Eitne's eye. She nodded back with a grin.

'I didn't know your brother could juggle,' said Lugach.

'I wouldn't call throwing three stones up into the air only for them to fall to the ground juggling,' Cana answered. 'But it seems to at least be holding Benandonner's attention. For now, anyway.'

As Iollan continued to kill time by performing for the giant, Eitne began to worry that her and Caicer's potion had not worked. That she had not correctly managed the careful balance of chamomile, valerian, wild lettuce and that secret something-else. After all, the giant had eaten a dozen bowls of soup filled with the magic potion prepared especially for him and was now halfway through the main course yet still seemed unaffected. Fionn, too, was beginning to think this plan was not going to work. And that he would have to resort to the sword and spear and find out just how skilled and strong this giant really was.

But then, suddenly Benandonner rose — half-angry, half-agitated. The cavern went silent. 'Fionn Mac Cumhaill,' he said. 'Where ... is ... this F-f-f- ...?'

The giant's head bobbed up and down, swung left and right. Then his whole frame seemed to sway and his legs quivered. His eyes widened and rolled back in his head, and he collapsed backwards, sending a table and its contents skywards.

'Thank goodness for that,' Fionn said. 'Well done, Eitne. How long have we got till he wakes?'

'I don't know, so I wouldn't be hanging around.'

'What now?' Lugach asked. 'Do we kill him?'

'We can't kill him,' Fionn replied. 'Not when he is asleep. It's not the Fianna way and would bring a curse on us. But don't worry, we've got a plan. Haven't we, Diorraing?'


'Urrghhh ... my head!' Benandonner slowly opened his eyes. Sitting up, he couldn't for the life of him remember where he was. But then a young man with fair hair sitting nearby caught his eye.

'Oh, good, you're awake,' Fionn said.

'Who are you?' the giant asked.

'Who am I? I'm Demne, of course. Do you not remember?'

Benandonner looked around. The more he saw, the more confusion spread across his face. 'Where am I?'

'In Fionn's house.'

'Who?'

'Fionn. Fionn Mac Cumhaill. You really must have drunk too much of that fine ale last night! This is the house of the great Irish giant Fionn Mac Cumhaill, the man you are going to fight to the death later.'

'What? Fight to the death? Why does he want to fight me?'

'He doesn't,' Fionn replied, sounding bemused. 'You want to fight him. You came here yesterday looking to have his head, but by the time Fionn came home you had fallen asleep.'

'That can't be true!' Benandonner said angrily.

'Ssshhh!' Fionn cut across him. 'You'll wake the baby.' But it was too late. From around the corner the sound of crying could be heard.

'What baby?' the giant said, suddenly embarrassed for the trouble he had caused.

'It's my master's.' As Fionn spoke, Diorraing toddled around the corner, or at least did the closest thing to a toddle he could muster. Dressed in the most baby-like outfit that the dressmakers of Tara could produce, Diorraing took one look at Benandonner and began to wail loudly.

'This is a baby?' the giant asked incredulously

'Isn't he gorgeous? Looks the very spit of Fionn, too, although he is not a year old.' As they both watched, Diorraing waddled over to one of the benches. He picked it up and smashed it against a wall. 'He's got his father's strength as well,' Fionn said.

'What's going on? Where is my baby?' The voice of a woman echoed in the cave.

'Oh no!' Fionn groaned. 'I was afraid this might happen – that's my master's wife, Oonagh. She is a monster in the morning when you wake her early. Look, you can see her beginning to rise.' Fionn pointed past the fire to where a curtain was pulled across. As Benandonner watched, the most enormous silhouette of a woman was lit up through the curtain. 'Quick, let's step out before she sees us.'

As they exited the cave, Cál approached on horseback. 'Good morning,' he announced. 'I have a delivery for Fionn Mac Cumhaill.'

'Excellent,' Fionn said. 'I was afraid it would be delayed.'

'What would be delayed?' Benandonner asked, his formerly loud and commanding voice threaded with uncertainty.

'Fionn's favourite knife. It had been blunted a moon ago when he slew a sea monster so it was being sharpened. It's his lucky knife, you see.' As he spoke, a team of horses came pulling an enormous cart that carried the longest knife that the blacksmiths of Tara would ever make.

'Th-th-that's a very big knife,' said Benandonner warily.

'Well, my master is a very big giant,' Fionn said. 'But he'll be back soon and you can see for yourself.'

After a few moments of silence, Benandonner, who was shifting uneasily from one foot to the other, spoke. 'Where is Fionn now?'

'Out for a swim, I suspect. He likes to get the blood circulating before a fight to the death. Why?'

'I ... I ... I can't wait any longer,' Benandonner shouted. 'I am the King of the Maelán and have been away long enough from my people. Tell Fionn he is lucky to have escaped my wrath this time, but never let him come to my Isle of Manau or he will be sorry. Do you hear that? He will be sorrrryyy!' Benandonner was still shouting back at them as he disappeared over the nearby hill.

The next day as they rode home they were still talking about the giant. 'Your granduncle Ros was right when he said they really weren't that smart,' Cana said.

'I know,' Fionn replied, astride the steed that he had since christened 'the Grey'. 'Thinking that you were Fionn's wife by the giant shadow you cast — and you were only sitting beside a candle!'

'Or that I was a baby,' Diorraing, who was trotting behind, added.

Iollan spoke. 'Well, those infant clothes did look kind of comfy on you.'

As Diorraing flushed with embarrassment, Ossnat flashed him a wink before speaking up. 'They did, Iollan. It was kind of you to lend them.'

As everyone erupted in laughter, Cana brought her horse to a halt.

'What?' Fionn asked.

'Look.' She pointed to a faint column of smoke in the distance of the still evening sky.

'Tara,' Fionn said, sparking into life. 'The palace is on fire! Come on! HYAH!'

# THE DARK DRUID

By the time Fionn and his fellow warriors reached Tara, the worst of the blaze had been put out, although some royal buildings were still smouldering. To Fionn's relief, Sadb ran straight out to meet them. She was quickly joined by the High King, Crimmal, Cnes, who had returned from the south, and several other Fianna warriors.

'Is everyone okay?' Fionn asked.

'We've had no reports of deaths yet,' said Art, 'though we won't know for sure for a few hours. Some people are still unaccounted for. The Chief Druid is currently being tended to by a healer. He is fine now, though he was nearly dead when he was pulled from his chambers by Sárait, along with his two sacred texts. He had a bad blow to the head, which I suppose occurred when he fell having been overcome with the smoke.'

'What happened?' Fionn continued.

'We don't know yet. It began yesterday around dusk. Yells and shouts alerted us. At first, we feared that we were under attack by Goll — or even the dragon back from the dead. But, in the light of day, it appears that it started in Caicer's chambers. They've been utterly destroyed. Maybe an invention gone wrong or potions that should not have been mixed.'

'An invention, my backside!' The group turned to see Caicer marching in, his head bandaged.

'Chief Druid, you should be lying down,' Sadb said.

'Plenty of time to lie down when I am dead,' he replied, before adding abruptly, 'Lachtna. It was Lachtna!'

At first, many did not understand. Some thought that their fellow warrior Lachtna, who had not been seen since before the fire, might have lost his life to the flames. But more devastating news was soon delivered. Lachtna had visited Caicer in his chambers the previous night. 'He said he wanted something to help him sleep, that he was still feeling sick. But there was something in the way he acted that, at first, I could not put my finger on. I suddenly got nervous in his company, sensing he wanted to do me harm. I realised my staff was on the far side of the room, and he saw me looking at it and smiled. I knew then he was not a friend. I remember little of what happened next. He must have struck me because I was lying on the floor. I could hear crackling and rustling and a dancing brightness coming first from my table and then from the drapes across the window. He was setting fire to the room. My last memory is of him hunkering down beside me, still smiling — and he was now holding my staff. "Someone wants this back," he said, before rising and walking out the door.' Caicer looked up to the High King. 'I'm sorry, I should have stopped him.'

'I should have known he was not a true Fianna warrior,' Fionn said. 'Any fault lies with me.'

'It's done,' Art said. 'You're alive, Caicer. That's what is important, and though he took your staff, he left the sacred books that Sárait managed to save for you.'

The Chief Druid turned to Sárait and thanked her. She grunted awkwardly in response — being thought of as anything other than fierce was a change for her.

'So someone wants the staff back,' said Art, thinking of Lachtna's parting words. 'Who?'

'Tadg,' Fionn said. 'Who else?'

Caicer nodded. 'That's what I believe.'

'If this is the work of Tadg,' Art said, 'then why did Lachtna leave the sacred texts?'

'The Book of Brega and the Book of Mag Tuired contain many powerful spells and incantations, but the Great Book of Moytura was always the most powerful and the one that Tadg favoured,' said Caicer.

'And it was never found after Tadg was banished.'

'No, it wasn't. I believe it lies hidden away in his old home of Almu. The staff that Lachtna took from me greatly increases the magical power of the one who wields it, for good or for bad. But it is sacred texts that truly give it strength. I believe Almu is where Lachtna is going.'

'Who is protecting it at the moment?' Fionn asked.

'Raigne,' said Cnes. 'He split off from our group as we travelled south last month and took over Almu's defence. His cousin Úaine is nearby at the crossroads of An Nás.'

'How many soldiers do they have?'

'No more than ten soldiers apiece.'

'Well, if Lachtna has allies with him and Tadg has returned and got his hands on the Chief Druid's staff, they are not safe. We'd better hurry.'

Some thirty miles to the south, a group of eight men were seated in the shadow of a steep ridge that hid their camp. One of these was Lachtna, and most of the others had until a week ago not set foot on the island of Ireland for more than three years. All the group were accomplished warriors with the exception of one, whom they referred to as the Dark Druid, though not to his face. Others knew him as Tadg, and while the warriors around him spoke in hushed tones, he was enthralled by the object in his hand. He had not held it in seventeen long winters. In all that time it had not lost its wonder.

The six-sided object was fashioned from a single chunk of pale-grey flint splashed with patches of brown and polished and decorated on every side. The Bóinne Mace Head was a thing of beauty. It was made long, long ago and had the highest level of artistry, with intricately carved spirals and lozenges. On one side, the carvings appeared to form a human face, with a wide, gaping mouth, where a wooden staff fitted. Growing up, he had heard old druids speak of how this face was one of awe and wonder, which reflected how people felt towards the magic that this staff could wield. For him, though, it was a face of fear, terror and dread, something he was sure that he would soon visit on anyone who would challenge him.

'What of the druid?' Tadg asked, bringing silence to the warriors.

'Dead,' Lachtna replied.

'Dead? Are you sure?'

Lachtna looked to the other warriors, who did not return his gaze. It had been a week since the boat that had carried them and Tadg had docked in the north-east.

A few days before, a giant had caused havoc a little further west and the distraction this had caused had helped ensure the arrival of six heavily armed men and a druid would not be noticed. While these warriors of Goll had travelled from the Isle of Manau to help Tadg, all were wary of him. It was as if a stench of evil surrounded him, which made them keep their distance when they could. Five miles east of Tara, Lachtna had joined them on their southward journey. And he immediately had the same feeling about the druid.

'I knocked him out and set fire to the whole building.'

'Ah, so you left him for dead. That's not the same thing as killing him, which is what you should have done.'

'Well, if we want to speak of leaving someone for dead and not killing them, before I left Tara word came that the giant you sent off to Ulster to kill Fionn had failed and was returning home.'

Tadg gave an ireful look that caused Lachtna to squirm. 'The spell I put on him was weak, and I did not expect it to succeed. I have higher expectations for you, so don't let me down again.' He changed the subject. 'How far are we from Almu?'

'No more than ten miles to our west.'

'So why did we stop?'

'Before we take Almu, there is a small garrison of soldiers at An Nás, just over that ridge. They are led by a Fianna warrior by the name of Úaine, whose cousin, Raigne, holds Almu. We can't risk her coming to his aid and attacking us from behind. Especially if Almu doesn't fall quickly. An Nás is more exposed and easier to take, so we go there first.'

Úaine looked down at the fidchell board. It was her move. For more than a month, she had been playing Raigne, with birds couriering their moves back and forth. She was a good player, a proper strategist, but Raigne had managed to outmanoeuvre her in the last two games of this Celtic chess, and she was in trouble again. 'Cousin, what are you trying to do?' she whispered under her breath.

'Úaine! Greetings!'

Úaine turned to see Lachtna approaching in the company of one of her soldiers. 'Ugh,' she thought. Few Fianna had any warmth for Lachtna and Úaine was no exception. Several times during their training she had confronted him because of the way he had treated others, putting him on his backside on at least one occasion. Still, he was now a fellow member of the Fianna and it was her duty to give welcome.

'Hello, Lachtna,' she said, embracing him briefly before retaking her seat. 'Any more news from Tara?'

'None,' Lachtna answered. 'Why do you ask?'

'I received word on the wing yesterday that there was a fire in the royal buildings and that we were to remain alert.'

'I had not heard,' Lachtna said, holding her gaze, unblinking. 'I've been travelling for a few days now.'

'Oh?' Úaine said. 'Where to?'

'South,' Lachtna replied curtly. He looked quickly to the fidchell board. 'Who's winning?'

'Raigne – it's starting to become a bit of a habit.'

'Where is he?' Lachtna asked.

'Almu.'

'Does he have many soldiers with him or any dogs?'

'Eight soldiers, I think, and the wolfhound Lombhall.' Úaine swivelled to face Lachtna. 'What's with the questions? And where in the south are you going exactly?'

Lachtna looked at her and then the fidchell board, smiling as he pointed. 'I can see why you're losing.'

'How?' Úaine asked, turning back to the game.

'Because you keep leaving yourself open.'

Úaine suddenly realised what Lachtna had meant, but it was too late. A sharp pain shot up from her back, where Lachtna had stabbed her. 'Coward!' she said through gritted teeth as Goll's forces sprang forth.

Raigne was sitting high up in the palace of Almu, feeling the warmth of the setting sun on his face. He knew any

102

danger that might come would likely be from the east, but on long summer's evenings like this it was impossible not to be held in thrall by the sunsets that the palace's height offered.

Raigne had volunteered to continue guarding Almu against the threat of the old Chief Druid. Both he and Úaine would have preferred to have been based along the coastline, a little closer to where they might expect more action. But blood-red summer sunsets and the closeness to his cousin were some compensation.

Raigne thought about Úaine. She had yet to send word of her next move and nearly a day had passed. It was unlike her. She was as quick-thinking as she was quick-tempered, and it was usually him who pondered over the next move. Raigne smiled to himself. That he had won the last couple of fidchell games was surely something that would be getting to her.

Words drifted up from below — the sound of someone familiar talking to his soldiers. It was hard to make out but it sounded like Lachtna.

Alongside Fionn rode Cana, Cnes, Iollan, Fiacha, Diorraing, Ossnat and Cál, with three times as many soldiers quick-marching behind, several hounds in tow, Sadb, with her healing powers, and a recent recruit by the name of Créde. When they got to an area known as the Flowing

Forest, they split into two bands. One group, led by Cana and including Cnes, Iollan and Cál, veered east to An Nás. Fionn and the others travelled west to Almu.

The woodland floor was speckled with bright light from where the canopy opened to allow the sunshine through. In these parts, grass and shrubs were at their highest, competing to climb and fill the gap that a fallen winter tree had vacated. Though it was late afternoon, the sound of birds echoed through the forest as the scents and aromas of a rich summer day filled the air. It was momentary respite from worry and the threat of conflict. But all too soon, Fionn emerged from the wooded cover to see the palace of Almu ahead of him.

While it had been abandoned for some time, it still held on to its former greatness, rivalling the High King's own palace in Tara. The building had not always been so grand. When it had been built it had been named after Tadg's wife. And, while the structure was always beautiful, it was much smaller. But when Tadg's wife died, having first become grievously ill after giving birth to Muirne — Fionn's mother — things changed. Tadg had turned to the dark magic of the Dealra Dubh, pledging his soul in a desperate and ultimately futile effort to save her life. It was then that he began to add to and embellish the palace of Almu, preferring to build on the memory of his dead wife than to care for his living daughter.

In his time as Fianna chief, Fionn had not once set foot inside these buildings. To him, they were filled with sadness and this visit was not going to change that.

In the main hall lay the body of his friend and fellow warrior Raigne. It was only lightly armed, as were many of the bodies of his fellow soldiers that were found around the palace. It appeared that whoever did this had been able to easily gain access to the building. 'Lachtna,' Fionn cursed under his breath.

As he knelt beside Raigne, Diorraing approached. 'We've found something you need to see.'

In a corner of the palace, a fissure was exposed. Beside it lay a great granite slab of such weight that a battalion of soldiers would find it hard to shift. Yet there it was, removed to reveal the opening of a souterrain — an underground chamber — which now lay empty.

'If this is where Tadg had hidden the Great Book of Moytura long ago, it has been found.'

'There's something else,' Diorraing said, leading Fionn to the body of an enemy warrior. Beside him was the hound Lombhall, who had been killed by several arrows.

Fiacha was standing beside the fallen warrior. 'Temnén,' he said.

'Who?' said Fionn.

'Temnén — one of Goll's men and someone I haven't seen in years.'

'Are you sure?'

'Certain.'

As they reflected on the news that Goll had once again joined the Dark Druid, Ossnat entered the room. 'We have found their tracks — several sets of horses' hooves.'

'Moving east, back to the coast?' Fionn asked.

'No, heading north-west.'

'North-west? Why go deeper into Ireland rather than escape?' He turned to Fiacha. 'Who is stationed up there for us?'

'I believe Iollan had Échna and Donn posted there to strengthen this length of coastline.'

'Were Raigne's messenger birds killed?'

'No, they are alive,' said Fiacha.

'Good, then send word to the forts where Échna and Donn might be stationed. Tell them to ready whatever soldiers they have to hand and march towards us.' As his commands were being carried out, Fionn put his thumb to his mouth and spoke quietly to himself. 'Just where are you going, Tadg?'

At the same time, a similar question was being posed by Lachtna. 'We have killed two Fianna warriors, more than a dozen men, and have set fire to the royal palace. Why are we not fleeing this island right now?'

Tadg turned to the young warrior. 'Because we are going to Rathcroghan.'

'Why?'

'I will raise an army for Goll Mac Morna there.'

'There hasn't been an army at the old royal seat of Rathcroghan in hundreds of years,' Lachtna said. 'It's a deserted fort!'

'It's not what is waiting in the fort but what is waiting underneath it.'

Lachtna looked confused.

'For a decade after the High King, Conn of the Hundred Battles, took everything from me I tried to regain my power, to connect again with the Dealra Dubh. I knew he resided in the Otherworld in a sidhe somewhere on this land. And for years I searched. With the help and greed of men and their lust for the gold and silver these sidhes contained, I opened one after another until I got to Rathcroghan. Deep in the hill where the ancient fort once stood I found a sidhe's entrance, a great monolithic slab of stone. I could feel the power of the Dealra Dubh behind it. But neither the thieves nor I could move it. The magic that had sealed it shut was too strong.

'I gave up and spent years in the wilderness until I heard of Goll's growing strength overseas. I knew this was my opportunity. Now, with the Bóinne Mace Head and the Great Book of Moytura, I am ready. The magic of Rathcroghan's seal will no longer protect it. I will open it, and when the great festival of Lughnasa occurs less than half a moon away, when Otherworldly spirits are at full strength, the forces of the Dealra Dubh will be released, and between the forces within and outside Ireland, the High King, Fionn and the Fianna will be crushed forever. No one will stand in our way. That, Lachtna, is why we are going to Rathcroghan.'

'I still don't get it.' Cnes was struggling with her horse again. In the weeks since the animals had been brought over from across the water, the Fianna warriors had become familiar to varying degrees with their larger and more highly strung steeds. Some, such as Cana and her chestnut horse, Agile, were like one mind in how they moved. Cnes, by contrast, on her own steed, Black Stream, appeared far from comfortable.

'You just need to relax,' Cana said.

'That's fine for you to say, but you are able to use that ...'

'Bridle and bit?'

'Yes, use that bride and bit with ease. I try the same thing, and it doesn't work.'

'It's called a bridle not a bride, for starters, and you still don't understand,' said Cana. 'You really just need to relax. Horses understand how you're feeling, and it makes them feel the same way. If you are nervous, they are nervous; if you're relaxed, they will be too.'

'He's twice the size of me — what has he to be nervous about?' Cnes replied.

Cana laughed. 'Because the person who is sitting on his back and is meant to be directing him thinks she doesn't know what she's doing. I'd be nervous too.'

As they spoke, Fionn rode down the convoy of Fianna warriors and soldiers, Conbec running alongside him, without even noticing Cana and Cnes. Both Fianna forces had reunited. And after burying the bodies of their fellow soldiers and warriors and laying stones atop their graves to mark their passing, they had proceeded in convoy north-westwards, with Luas and Cuaird's noses leading the way.

'Hi, Fionn,' Cnes said jokingly as he disappeared behind. 'Not very friendly today.'

'Don't be too tough on him,' said Cana. 'As leader, I think he feels personally to blame for the deaths of Úaine and Raigne.'

A short time later, Fionn, with Conbec, galloped past Cana and Cnes, again without a word, before he drew up his steed beside Sadb.

'At least he has time to speak to someone,' Cnes said.

'I am glad he does. Being a leader of such a force can't be easy.'

'You're not jealous, then?' Cnes enquired.

'Jealous? Jealous of what?'

'Of the fact that Fionn is opening himself up, not to you but to Sadb.'

Cana laughed.

'Well?'

'Well what?'

'Well, you still haven't answered my question,' Cnes said playfully.

Cana looked at Fionn. 'I always saw him like a brother and nothing more, to be honest.'

'Really?' Cnes smiled.

'Yes, really. Now speaking of brothers and about love, which is what you are clearly trying to talk about, what of my brother? Seems like you two have spent long enough making fun of each other. Any thoughts on whether you might say something nice to each other for a change?'

Cnes smiled again, this time blushing a little. 'It's true. I don't dislike him.'

'That's lucky, because I know Iollan doesn't dislike you a lot.'

'Did he say anything?' Cnes said eagerly.

'He's my brother,' Cana answered. 'I know when he is in love. And he isn't the only one, you know.'

'Why, who else?'

'Look back at Diorraing. You'll see him riding alongside Ossnat. That deep affection is more than a year old now. Just past them is Cál. Since we left Tara he has been in constant conversation with a woman from your part of the country.'

'Who?' Cnes asked, intrigued by all these tales of young love.

'Her name is Créde. She has been ably helping Eitne Ollamda, Sadb and Caicer with the sick and the wounded. The cloak Cál is wearing is one she made for him.'

'Who would have known?'

'Indeed,' Cana said, looking at Fionn and Sadb. 'Who would have known.'

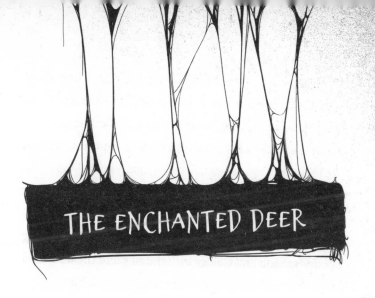

# THE ENCHANTED DEER

From between two conifers Donn had a full view of the mound of Rathcroghan. It was a steep hill about forty metres in diameter, which still contained remnants of the old military fort it once held, surrounded by concentric earthen embankments that radiated outwards. The hill was marked by standing stones, dotted with elder trees and covered largely by spindle and whitethorn. It had been many generations since the hill had been the site of a fort of great splendour. As a young boy, Donn had been mesmerised by tales of the queen who had inhabited it and who had once reigned over these lands from this seat of power. There were other stories of a female spirit who moved from one world to another through a sidhe hidden deep in the foundations of the fort. For years the fort had been abandoned and the sidhe sealed shut. However, now the outlines of armed figures could be seen on the mound.

About fifty yards ahead, halfway between Donn and the hill, Échna was slowly crawling forward, the shield strapped to her back giving her a beetle-like appearance. She was creeping along just under the crest of the second-nearest embankment. A large black rook looked down on her from an elder tree, seemingly unperturbed by this human visitor.

Word had come from Fionn only a couple of days before to where they had been stationed along the shell-strewn coast of what would become known as Sligo. They had been instructed to take their forces south-east to intersect an enemy incursion that contained Tadg and the traitor Lachtna.

After reaching a village by the name of Wet Hill, they heard from the locals about the passing through of seven men — each as threatening as the next — heading north-west. They must have just missed each other. Échna, Donn and their forces turned back and soon found horse tracks that branched left, which they followed to the ancient fort of Rathcroghan.

Échna had won the game of Rock, Spear and Cloth, which was why she was now leading a dozen soldiers up the mound to Lachtna and his men, while Donn spread his troops around the hill to prevent their enemies' escape.

She was visible to Donn, but the crest of the embankment would hide her from Lachtna's warriors. Suddenly, though, something seemed off. Despite Échna's concealed position, there was a flurry of motion on the hill.

'Have they noticed her?' Donn whispered to himself.

They had. Weapons were pointing towards his Fianna friend. Échna guessed that something had given her position away. Knowing the surprise was up, she rose to attack. Her group might not have had the strongest position, but they had the numbers. Standing up and bearing her shield for protection, she gave a western war-cry from the island of her birth. Her soldiers came to her side and they charged forward. But as she yelled, Lachtna, with a sure and cruel cast, sent a spear towards her, shattering Échna's shield and impaling her.

From high above, Lachtna marvelled at the sheer strength of his throw. As he watched Échna's body being dragged back by the retreating Fianna soldiers, a voice came from behind him.

'You see? The awesome strength of the Dealra Dubh!'

Just as Échna had been advancing on the fort of Rathcrohgan, Tadg had emerged from a dark recess to alert Lachtna and his men that they had been surrounded.

He had then enchanted Lachtna's spear with some words from his sacred text. The result had been devastating.

'I am nearly there. The sidhe is almost open,' Tadg said. 'I can feel it.'

'Good,' Lachtna replied, pointing to the south. 'Because it looks like we have more company.'

As the new band of Fianna warriors approached, the unmistakable fair hair of their champion could be seen. 'Fionn,' Lachtna said, but he didn't have to tell Tadg. While the druid might never have set eyes on the young man, he knew it was his grandson.

Fionn also knew who was now looking at him from several hundred yards away. The stooped, slight figure of an old man could only be the Dark Druid, his grandfather Tadg.

'Greetings, Donn.' Fionn hailed his fellow warrior as he came to meet him. 'And Échna?' Donn's crestfallen face gave him his answer. For the second day in a row, Fionn felt a heavy weight drag on his stomach as Donn began to recount the circumstances of another friend's death.

'What now?' Lachtna asked. 'Is the Dealra Dubh strong enough to enchant more weapons against such a number?'

'No,' Tadg answered flatly, turning back towards the hollow. 'But it won't take me much longer.'

'What if they attack while you're down there?'

'Don't worry, I'll know.' As Tadg descended into the dark, a black rook flew from its perch and began circling high above Rathcroghan.

Fionn was silent. He sat with the top of his thumb in his mouth, thinking and listening. Cana, Cnes, Fiacha, Ossnat and the others had all given their counsel, yet he still could not make up his mind. Decisions that had once been clear had, with the deaths of his friends, suddenly become shrouded in uncertainty.

'Darkness is beginning to fall,' he said. 'Let's make camp and I will think on what course is best to take.'

'That's it?' Cana asked, surprised at Fionn's hesitancy. 'They've killed three of our friends!'

'I know,' Fionn snapped, 'and I don't want to lose any more.'

'So — what? We should just sit here and wait while Tadg is doing who-knows-what up there?'

Fionn was silent, and stayed silent even when Cana left in anger, with the other warriors dispersing soon after.

He remained seated for some time afterwards in the growing darkness, biting his thumb, lost in thought, robbed of ideas. He might have sat there the whole night if not for Sadb.

'What is it, Fionn? What's wrong?' she said, clasping his hands in her own and taking a seat beside him. Not for the first time, Fionn noticed the softness of her hands. He thought of how their tenderness must bring great relief to the sick, the injured and the dying. Returning the strength of their grip, he looked up to her with eyes full of sorrow and fear. 'For once in my life, I don't know what to do. Cana is right. Who knows what Tadg is doing up there? But if I go, how many more of my friends will die? You heard Donn's account of Échna's death. That's dark magic at play, and it is powerful.'

Sadb remained silent.

'What would you do?'

'I am not a warrior,' she answered. 'I don't fight, at least not in the way you or the Fianna do. I believe there are always other ways than violence. But that is my path, and that doesn't help you. You are currently on another path, where the decisions are different.'

'What if I can't decide?'

'But you can,' Sadb replied. 'Every moment you are deciding. Staying put is a decision. Fighting is a decision. They are all decisions, whether you think so or not. You just need to take responsibility for them. That's what being a leader is about.'

Fionn looked into her eyes, and though it was now dark, he could really see her. 'I love you, you know that?'

'I know.' She said, kissing him gently. 'Now, I have to get ready for whatever decision you make.'

'Can I ever change paths?' Fionn asked, just as Sadb rose to leave.

'We can always change paths,' she smiled.

'Don't get too comfortable,' Fionn said, approaching Cana, Cnes and Iollan, who were in the process of making camp for the night.

'Why?' Cana asked, irritation still in her voice.

'Because you were right. We don't know what Tadg is up to – but there is one way to find out.'

At this, Cana smiled. 'Good, let's get ready then.'

'Wake anyone who is sleeping,' Tadg, emerging from the dark recess, barked to Lachtna.

'What's going on?'

'They are getting ready to attack,' the Dark Druid replied.

'And what about the sidhe?'

'Don't worry,' Tadg said. 'Fionn and his warriors are too late – it has been opened.'

'Where are they, then?' Lachtna asked, looking past Tadg to the entrance of the sidhe. 'Where are the spirits that are going to attack and defeat the Fianna?'

'It doesn't work like that. I've already said we must wait until Lughnasa. But they will come, do not worry. Now, I need you to tell me something. There is a woman to whom Fionn speaks, a young woman with long blond hair who isn't dressed for war.'

'Sadb,' Lachtna said. 'She's a healer and has his heart. They are in love and have been for the last year.'

'That's what I thought. I want you to bring this love of his to me.'

'We are surrounded by them. How do you –?'

'Just listen carefully and I will guide you.'

Cál was kneeling in the dark, waiting for the call. In one hand he held the Brave and Quick Wounding, a spear bewitched by an ancient magic that had been passed down through his family for generations and had always served him. In his other hand, a sword. His love, Créde, would ask him to carry a shield, but that was not his way of fighting. He joked that not having a shield meant he would be reunited with her more quickly. But she hated such humour. 'I never want to have to try to heal you,' she would chastise him.

He knew, from what happened to Échna, that although the enemy warriors lying in wait at Rathcroghan were few, there was a dark magic behind them. For once, he felt a tremor of worry. It was hard not to. But he tried not to show it, even though Créde had noticed it earlier when they were preparing for battle. She always knew how he was feeling.

Cál was still smiling at the thought of Créde when Fionn's war-cry rang out for his warriors, soldiers and hounds to attack. For everyone, there was nothing else to do now except prepare for battle and face the danger of Tadg, Lachtna and his men.

As she led the charge from the eastern side, Cana was glad it was a cloudy, moonless night. Every so often she heard the hiss of an arrow and a shout from someone who had been hit. However, the darkness had helped cloak their attack.

Ahead of her, the roar of a warrior signalled the first engagement with the enemy. A moment later, she began battle with another. Cana knew the dangers that lay in front of her. But she trusted her skills as a warrior and took confidence in that it was one thing she could control. It helped her to focus and drove her to defeat the first of Lachtna's men. She wrong-stepped her opponent. He drew forward and missed, which allowed her to pierce his unprotected midriff.

By the time her first adversary had fallen, the battle was white-hot. Sharp sounds of metal striking metal and shouts, roars and howls filled the night air. It was then that Cana glimpsed Fionn shooting past. It surprised her. Fionn was to attack from the western flank, and for a moment she wondered had he gone astray. 'Fionn!' she shouted, but he was gone. And then the holler of her brother Iollan called her back to the fray.

'Fionn. Are you hurt?'

Sadb was surprised to see Fionn's blank face staring at her through the entrance of the tent in which she and Créde were ready to treat the injured. Shouts and screams could be heard from the hilltop. Sadb and Créde would soon be needed. But Fionn was there first. He beckoned her outside.

'What is it? What's happened?' Sadb asked, checking Fionn for blood or a sign of injury, of which there was none.

Then she realised. Although she had been staring at someone who looked just like Fionn, his eyes were those of a stranger. Suddenly the deception ended and it was not Fionn standing there but Lachtna, grinning wickedly. Dark magic had enabled him to look and appear as her love. Before she could react, Lachtna struck her hard across the temple, knocking her out cold. A moment later, he had taken a horse, thrown her limp body across it and was riding away to the north.

The Dark Druid opened his eyes and smiled malevolently. His work here was done. The sidhe was open and Sadb had been taken. The warriors holding the line could continue, but they would do so alone. It was time for him to go and follow Lachtna. The Fianna were closing in. He approached one of the horses. Taking two blood-red cloths from inside his tunic, he tied one on the tail of his steed before tying another around his own upper arm. He mounted the horse, closed his eyes and then, from the Great Book of Moytura opened in front of him, he called forth an incantation. But before the Fianna had reached the summit of the hill, Tadg, wrapped in his cloak of invisibility, had vanished.

As the last of Lachtna's warriors were defeated a strange sort of silence descended on the hill, save for the groans of those who had been wounded. Cana approached the summit, relieved to see her friends alive and well, including Fionn.

'How did you get back here so quickly?' she said, embracing him.

'What do you mean?'

'You passed me by at the start of the battle. I called you but you kept going.'

'No, I didn't.'

They looked at each other, trying to understand who was wrong. And then they heard the calls of a woman in distress.

Cál was the first to hear Créde's account of what had happened to Sadb and first to begin the pursuit.

He had struggled to find the trail, so he trusted blind luck and made a beeline for the north-western coast. His guess was rewarded. After a few hours of riding his steed, Dianras, near the great limestone outcrop known as the Hill of the Stripes, he saw two horses ahead of him. On one rode a smaller figure. On the other, the larger frame of a warrior, holding a much slighter body. It was certainly the trio of Tadg, Lachtna and Sadb. Cál was gaining but he knew that the riders ahead would still reach the Bay of Leathros before he could catch them. 'Go, Dianras!' he shouted, driving his horse onwards while above him the towering clouds of an incoming squall approached.

A few miles behind Cál, Fionn was also moving fast. With him were Cana, Cnes, Iollan and Ossnat. Ossnat and the hounds had helped pick up the trail and the group had made good ground. With Fionn's horse, the Grey, more suited to the tough, undulating terrain of this part of the country, Fionn soon pulled ahead. 'Be careful!'

Cana shouted as the distance between them lengthened. By the time the smell of sea air had reached them, both Fionn and the Grey had disappeared.

It was unusual to have such weather in late summer, with powerful updraughts heralding a violent rainstorm. 'Quick, take her down and get her aboard,' Tadg barked at Lachtna as they reached the froth-covered waves churned up by the sudden gusts. Meeting them were a brace of sailors loyal to Goll. They took Sadb, now conscious but bound, towards a ship waiting in the bay. As the dark, foreboding skies opened with rain that quickly became a deluge, the Dark Druid wrapped a crimson cloth around Lachtna's upper arm. 'This will make you invisible to others. Strike down any who threaten us as we clear the shallows, and then rejoin us.' No sooner had Tadg turned from the ship than a horse and rider emerged from the machair dunes and galloped towards them. It was Cál.

Through the biting sand whirling around him, Cál could see the ship being loaded. It was hard to make out the faces, but as he galloped towards them he could see Sadb's body being brought aboard – followed by Tadg's unmistakable stooped frame. 'Yah!' Cál shouted as he encouraged his horse forwards once more.

Sadb could feel her hair stuck to her brow, now caked with blood. While her head still throbbed from where Lachtna had struck her, the ache had subsided somewhat. But she was still grimacing, in part due to the pain she was forcing on herself as she tried to wrestle her wrists free from the cords she was bound with. And in part due to the dread she now felt for Cál, whom she could see dismounting in the distance, oblivious to the trap he was walking into.

In the driving rain, the howling wind and the crashing waves, Cál did not hear Sadb's muffled screams, nor could he have known that Lachtna was advancing towards him, his sword raised. Instead, all Cál could see in his mind's eye was the straight, true throw of his spear that would finally vanquish his evil enemy, this Dark Druid. But as he drew back his arm, he saw Tadg standing proudly aboard the ship, staring intensely back at him. A fleeting thought crossed his mind. *Lachtna?*

By the time Fionn scrambled down to the beach, Cál's body was face down at the edge of the water, and the ship halfway out of the bay. Though the rain almost shrouded him, Tadg could be seen standing aboard and staring back at Fionn.

'Kill him,' Tadg whispered to himself. 'Kill him, Lachtna, kill him.'

Lachtna was still standing over Cál's body. He knew the ship would soon be out of reach, but here was Fionn of the Fianna and the hated Clan Bascna. Years ago, Lachtna had become a nobody. He had given up his family name of Mac Morna, had joined the Fianna and fed information back to his uncle Goll. Lachtna had been brought up on stories of all the wrongs that Clan Bascna had visited on his family and their hand in the tragedies of Clan Morna. As Fionn neared, unaware of his presence, Lachtna now had an opportunity to exact revenge.

He bent down and took Cál's spear, blanketing its visibility with his touch. The magic of the weapon and the strength of Tadg's power coursed through him once more. Fionn was less than twenty yards away and still oblivious to Lachtna's presence. Only his hound, Conbec, sensed something was wrong and began to growl and bark viciously.

'Kill him,' Tadg urged, his eyes fully possessed of evil, staff in hand, pointing towards them. 'Kill him.'

Lachtna lifted the spear skywards and cast it towards Fionn, with the strength of every sinew he possessed. But as he did, Fionn's eyes widened and he lurched to the side, preventing the full force of the spear from connecting with his heart. Instead, it struck him in the abdomen. Fionn collapsed, severely injured but still alive.

Lachtna cursed. Fionn had seen him at the last moment. He turned to the ship and could just about make out the figure of Sadb in the waves, swimming towards the shore. Tadg was cradling his arm in pain. She must have distracted the Dark Druid, breaking the crimson cloth's magic and making Lachtna visible once again. Swearing that a dagger would await her in the shallows, Lachtna turned back to Fionn and the growling mutt that now stood protecting him.

'Curse you,' Tadg screamed, deep toothmarks across his hand from where Sadb had bitten him. 'Where is it?' he shouted, desperately looking for his magical staff. The mace head rumbled as it rolled along the floor of the ship. The tempest grew in intensity. By the time he found it, Sadb was already a dozen yards away, swimming for shore. He knew that if he or the Dealra Dubh could not have her, neither would Fionn. She was a healer. He knew all healers had both powers and weaknesses. So, with her one weakness in mind, he conjured up an evil spell and cast it upon her.

Conbec was a brave, fierce dog. But Lachtna knew his own ability as a swordsman would end the life of this hound with one cold bite of metal. And then he would do the same for his master. But as he approached the dog and the prone body of Fionn, he heard a sudden, sharp *twang*. From his chest came a searing pain. A moment later, Lachtna collapsed on the sand, a spear through his torso, and the sound of familiar voices up ahead.

Sadb was near exhaustion when she felt the sand under her and began to lift herself out of the waves. She saw the motionless body of her love lying on the strand. Cana, Cnes, Iollan and others were approaching him. She sprinted towards them but, as she did, the hounds of the Fianna who had just arrived charged in her direction. She shouted, but no words left her. And still the hounds were running. Something primal took hold of her and suddenly she was bounding away at a speed she had never known.

'Fionn!' Cana shouted, crashing down on the sand beside him. 'He's alive – just! What of the others?'

Iollan ran out to Cál. But it was too late and he shook his head in sadness to the others. Cnes squatted beside Lachtna, gripping her spear that had pierced him. Lachtna grimaced.

'Sadb,' she said forcefully. 'Where is she?'

'In the water,' Lachtna whispered quietly, life and blood draining from him.

Cnes stood up and looked out. The squall, as quickly as it had descended, had disappeared. The ship was now far out to sea, and Cnes cursed their slowness in reaching the shore. To her right, the most unusual sight was playing out — Luas and Cuaird had joined two more hounds giving chase to a deer that must have been disoriented in the storm and strayed onto the beach. Only Conbec stayed put, whimpering as he looked at Fionn. 'Don't worry, boy. He'll be okay,' she reassured him.

'I don't see her,' Cnes said, crouching back down beside Lachtna — but by then he was dead. And a moment later Sadb, in the form of a deer, had disappeared too.

# THE QUEST OF CANA

'How is he doing?'

'He's dying.'

The room was silent, save for the laboured breathing of Fionn.

At the foot of his bed lay Conbec, who had not left his side from the time he had been wounded. Surrounding them were Cana, Cnes and Iollan. It had taken them a day and a half to bring Fionn's badly injured body back to Tara, where he could be treated, and they were all exhausted. Beside them stood the High King, the Chief Druid and Crimmal. Given the chance, every warrior in Tara would have waited beside their champion, but Eitne and Créde, who were tending to him, needed space to work. Fionn was fighting for his life, a fight that Eitne believed he was losing.

'Can he not be saved?' Crimmal asked. 'I've seen older and weaker men with worse wounds who've survived.'

'His injury is bad,' Eitne answered, 'but that's not what is killing him. It is the fact that it was Cál's spear that wounded him.'

'Any man who has been bloodied by it will die within nine days,' the High King said, repeating the well-known saying associated with the spear.

'I thought that was just legend,' said Iollan.

'I wish it was,' Eitne replied.

'But surely there must be some remedy?' Cana asked.

'There is, but not on this island.'

'Where then? Overseas?'

'No, down below in the Otherworld,' Eitne said. 'It is a Tuatha Dé Danann spear. Their magic enchanted it. And only their magic can now cure him.'

'The Tuatha? The spirits and gods whose monsters we spent a half-year slaying? Of whom the Dealra Dubh is one? They won't help us. And they certainly won't help Fionn.'

'They might,' Eitne said.

'Why?' asked Cana.

Eitne looked to Créde, who nodded back at her. 'Because some of us have the blood of the Tuatha Dé

Danann in our veins,' Eitne said. 'And we know that they are not all monsters.'

'Healers?' Cnes asked.

'Yes, most of us healers have their blood running through us,' Eitne replied. 'That's why we know the plants, flowers and herbs of this land so well. It is the blood – and the knowledge – of the Tuatha Dé Danann that taught us.'

'Sadb too?'

'Yes, Sadb too. For some, it is a distant ancestor who was of the Tuatha. Sadb was raised by her aunt, but her father was the Tuatha spirit Cernunnos, and that is why her healing was so strong. Maybe if she were here now, she could save Fionn.'

'But she's not,' Cana said solemnly. 'So what can we do, then? How do we get down there to find this cure?'

'I don't know.'

The High Druid, who had been listening intently, finally spoke. 'Maybe there is someone who does.'

'Well, if you have a plan, you need to act quickly,' Eitne said. 'Two days have already passed. He has only seven more, at most.'


The old man was sitting in the shade of a willow, fishing rod in hand. Small and bearded, he could have been a hundred years old.

Cana was first to step out from the clearing. 'What's the fishing like?'

'I haven't caught a fish in years.'

'Would you be better off using a boat? You might have more luck further out in the water.'

'I used to, but I kept falling in. As you get older, you prefer to take fewer risks, not more. You must be Cana.'

'I am.'

'Which means the young woman behind you is Cnes, the young man next to her Iollan. Chief Druid Caicer, I recognise well, and this other fellow ...?'

'Cailte.'

'Ah yes, Cailte, the great storyteller.'

'I tell stories, but I wouldn't call myself great.'

'In time, young man, in time.'

'You must be Finnegas, then?' said Cana. 'The great poet who taught Fionn all he knew.'

'I am Finnegas the poet. Although the Salmon of Knowledge probably played a larger role in Fionn's wisdom than I did.'

'How did you know we were coming?'

'I listen. Sometimes you Fianna are so busy with life's problems you don't slow down enough to take in everything. As you can see, I am not that busy any more. I have plenty of time and I hear enough news from the world around me.'

'Well, if you know who we are, then you probably know why we have come.'

'Yes. You are Fionn's friends and, like any good friends, you want to save his life. And you are looking for my help.'

'Will you give it?'

Finnegas reeled in his fishing line and laid the rod on the ground. He stood up, straightening his back as best he could. 'If I can, I will. What is it you want to know?'

'The Tuatha Dé Danann — can they really save him?'

'If you are asking me whether the cure to his sickness lies in the Otherworld, then the answer is yes. In the Otherworld is a tree called the Great Rowan Tree of Dubhros. Berries, deep scarlet in colour, grow on it. It is said that any who eat just three of them will be free from sickness and injury. They will cure Fionn. But if you are asking me if they are willing to give the berries to you, I don't know. That's something you will need to find out for yourself.'

'How do we get there? Through a sidhe?'

'Yes, but not any sidhe. There are many sidhes in this land, as you well know, but most are dead-ends — caves, really — where some monster or spirit of the Tuatha has been trapped with no means of escape. To the Otherworld proper, there are just two portals: one for those who are the enemies of people and one for those who are not.'

'Our friends, then?' Cnes asked.

'No.' Finnegas smiled wryly. 'I wouldn't call them our friends, exactly; they are just not our enemies. As you know, the Tuatha Dé Danann were the traditional foes of humans. When our ancestors, the Milesians, first arrived in Ireland, the leaders of the Tuatha were unwilling to live with them in peace. Instead, they led their kind into war. After much bloodshed, a sacred truce was brokered. But the leaders of the Tuatha betrayed their kind, who desired peace, and broke it. This brought defeat and disgrace upon them and forced all Tuatha into the Otherworld, where they were led by a new leader, Manannán Mac Lir. Some did come back to visit our lands, usually in animal form so they would not be noticed. This they did out of curiosity and kinship. Some of them found love and stayed, at least for a time.'

'And this is where the healers came from — Créde, Eitne, Sadb?'

'Yes, and many others too.'

'Why did these Tuatha not stay?' asked Cailte.

'Because this land is now ruled by humans, and if they stayed their lives would be shaped by the laws that humans are bound by, and they would lose their power.'

'What power?'

'The power of everlasting life. The Tuatha Dé Danann can live for ever. It is what sets them apart.

When peace was finally agreed and they left for the Otherworld, humans did not just inherit the earth, they brought their own natural laws with them.'

'Why does the Dealra Dubh continue to disrupt the lives of the living, then?' Iollan asked.

'He does more than disrupt. The Dealra Dubh will not stop until he sees the destruction of humankind. He is one of the Tuatha Dé Danann who never accepted their exile into the Otherworld. He wants them to return to these lands and is bent on our destruction. And he is not alone.'

'Wonderful,' Cnes said dryly. 'And what of the other Tuatha? What are they bent on?'

Finnegas smiled. 'They are not bent on anything. They just want to continue their lives in peace. And that is why the Otherworld is divided in two. The Tuatha who want revenge reside in one part. Those who respect the truce live in another. But both halves of their underworld kingdom can be accessed from our own.'

'Let me guess,' Cana said, 'the part where the Dealra Dubh lives can be reached through the sidhe of Rathcroghan?'

'Yes,' said Finnegas. 'How did you know?'

'Well, I guess your little friends who tell you the news have missed a few headlines. Only a few days ago we met Tadg and fought forces loyal to him and Goll at that sidhe.'

'That is not good,' Finnegas said, his face betraying concern.

'No, it's not. But what of the other entrance? Where is it?'

'Uisneach. The Hill of Uisneach. It is hidden under a great knot of limestone buried a hundred yards below the summit of the hill.'

'That's where the final truce between the Milesians and Tuatha Dé Danann was agreed,' Caicer said.

Finnegas nodded. 'And where you druids like to celebrate Bealtaine and the birth of summer every year. But ...' He hesitated.

'But what?' Cana asked.

'But if you do find the entrance and pass through it you will reach the Idir, a body of water that divides this world from theirs. You won't be able to swim through it, and if you try, you will never reach the far shore.'

'So how do we cross?'

'Abcán, the great Tuatha Dé Danann poet. He is the only one with a boat, and he decides who crosses.'

'Do you think he will help us?'

'I don't know. He can be a cantankerous old fool.'

'That doesn't sound positive,' Cana said.

'It isn't, but he is the friendliest Tuatha there – and you haven't any other options.'

'And if he does bring us across?'

'Then you are on your own. You'll have to find the tree and hope that the rest of the Tuatha allow you to live long enough to bring the berries back.'

'It all comes down to time,' Crimmal said. In front of him was a map and crowded around him were the High King, Caicer, Eitne, Cana, Cnes, Iollan and Cailte. Ernamis had also joined them, though her heart still weighed heavy following the death of her sister. 'Fionn was injured two days ago, giving him a week at most.' Eitne nodded in agreement. 'Tadg left at the same time. Ernamis, you know the western waters better than anyone. How long would it take the Dark Druid to round Ulster and make it back to the Isle of Manau, where reports say Goll and his fleet of ships are waiting for him?'

'Such a trip could take weeks, longer if the weather went against you,' Ernamis said.

'What if you could control the weather?' Cana asked. 'We all saw that tempest come in against us on the beach, yet the ship in which Tadg travelled was unaffected and the wind brought him out of the bay. What if Tadg can control the elements? How long would it take with the wind behind you the whole way?'

'A week, maybe less.'

'And with the Isle of Manau a good day and a half sail from here, in the right conditions, Goll, Tadg and their men could be landing on our beaches just as Fionn takes his last breath. Either way, we don't have much time.'

'Who will go?' Art asked Cana.

'Cnes and I will go,' she replied.

'Well, if you are going to the Otherworld, you should take this,' Crimmal said, holding out Fionn's treasure bag to Cana. 'If you are ever under threat, it will help. Fionn would want you to have it.'

Word was sent on the wing of a bird for any soldiers and clans close to Uisneach to find the knot of limestone Finnegas had spoken about and uncover it. Meanwhile, Cnes and Cana travelled through the night. By the time they arrived, the cairn had been found and was almost uncovered. A few hours later it was ready. A great monolith lay atop two enormous slabs of rock, between which a deep, dark crevice could be seen.

They slowly pressed their way into the crevice, where it got darker and darker and darker. The blacker it got, the tighter the passage felt, until the sides of it pressed in on them. But with great effort and determination and no little sweat they both managed to squeeze through. The passage widened and a light led them out. When they emerged they were met by a different type of illumination from the outside world, a silvery moon-like one. In front of them lay the calm waters of the Idir, but an impenetrable mist hung over it and blocked their view of the other side.

'What now?' Cana asked.

'I guess we wait?' said Cnes.

'Seemingly not,' Cana replied, pointing.

From out of the fog, a small currach appeared. And a man, smaller than Finnegas, if that were even possible, rowed towards them.

'Abcán?' Cana asked.

'Yes,' the old man replied, bringing his boat to a stop at the water's edge. 'Who are you and what do you want?'

'I am Cana, and this is Cnes. We are of the Fianna and we would like to cross.'

'Why?'

'The Great Rowan Tree of Dubhros is on the other side. Our friend is sick, and only the berries from that tree can save him.'

'Who sent you here?' Abcán asked.

'Finnegas,' Cnes said, beginning to lose her temper with all this delay. 'And he said you can be a cantankerous old fool who is unlikely to help us, so if you wouldn't mind not wasting our time and just telling us whether you'll bring us across or not.'

Cana glared at her.

'Too much?' she asked.

Abcán began laughing and didn't stop for some time. 'Oh, I miss humans.'

'Is that a yes, then?' Cana said.

'Yes, but I can only take one of you across. These are the rules and I can't change them. Only one person can cross the Idir.'

The friends looked at each other, sad that they could not go on together but in full agreement. Cana would go.

As they entered the mist, Cana spoke. 'Cnes was wrong when she said Finnegas thought you wouldn't help us.'

'But I'm sure she was right about the cantankerous part. How is Finnegas?'

'He seems happy.'

'That's good.' Abcán paused. 'I didn't mean to offend asking all those questions back there. I have taken three warriors across and, sadly, none of them has come back alive.'

'Did they come back at all?' Cana asked wryly.

'No.' Abcán chuckled. 'I guess they didn't come back at all.'

'How do you know they are dead, then?'

He turned to her with a look that answered that question. 'I see you have Manannán's treasure bag,' he said.

Cana looked down to the satchel Crimmal had given her as she left for Uisneach. 'It was Fionn's. It helped to keep him safe ... most of the time.'

'It is good you have it — you'll need it.'

Soon the mist cleared and they were across to the other side. They passed two towers of great volcanic-like rock that rose from the water and entered a crescent-shaped bay. Surrounding them on every side were great cliffs that swept down to a beach of black stones and sand, where they came ashore.

Abcán led Cana along the beach to where a river cut through it and the cliffs and connected to the Idir. Here another boat lay waiting. 'This is where I must leave you,' he said. 'We call this place the Meeting of the Waters, where this river flows in and out of the Idir and where, through those cliffs, it divides in two. Where it goes right, it travels to the shores of the capital of the Tuatha Dé Danann, where the great Bodb Derg now rules. The most powerful Tuatha Dé Danann live there. It is not a place you are welcome — and if they know you are here, they may not let you leave. The left will take you to where your treasure lies — to the Great Rowan Tree of Dubhros where the berries that will cure Fionn grow.

'So, I just need to sail down the river, climb the tree and get them?' Cana asked.

Abcán laughed. 'I'm afraid it is not that easy. The tree divides the Otherworld. On the far side of it is where the Dealra Dubh and all those who wish destruction on you and your people live. Protecting the tree and keeping the two sides of the Tuatha apart is a spirit of the Tuatha Dé Danann named Searbhann, a giant cyclops, hideous and foul to behold. All the Tuatha Dé Danann fear his strength. To get the berries you must get past Searbhann.'

'That sounds like a big ask,' Cana said.

'And I am afraid it gets worse before it gets better.'

'What's worse than a cyclops?' Cana asked.

'The three warriors who came here long ago for the same thing never got past what lies between you and the tree. That's what's worse. On this river you will pass the merrows. They are a coven of sea-maidens, women from the waist up but with fish-like tails from the waist down. They will call you with song as you travel along the river, hoping to draw you to shore, where your boat will be dashed against the rocks and the whirlpools will drag you down.

'If by a miracle you survive that, your boat will find land, but it is barren earth you will meet first. You must cross this bleak patch of land to reach the woodland where the Tree of Dubhros grows — but on the way you will have to pass the Suileach — a monster of a thousand eyes whose mouth spits venom.'

'Great,' said Cana. 'Mermaids that call me to my death, a venom-spewing monster with a thousand eyes and then a giant with one. Got it — shouldn't be too hard then!'

Very soon after, Cana was in the boat, moving upstream. It didn't seem possible for water to run this way, but it did, and soon enough the most enchanting music she had ever heard began to float down to her.

Abcán had not mentioned how beautiful the merrows were, sitting along the shore, each one combing her hair, smiling and singing a song that ...

Cana suddenly caught herself. It felt as if she had fallen asleep, but in her half-sleep she had begun rowing for shore. She swore not to let herself be dragged off again. But there was something in the music that ...

Once again, Cana wakened from a stupor — closer now to the shore, alarmed that she had once again dropped asleep. She began to bite her lip, hoping pain would keep her eyes open, but the tune kept coming and she could hear the rhythmic chants that the merrows ...

Cana was rowing hard and fast, ice in her blood as she managed to just draw back from the rocks. The merrow closest to her smiled and bared her teeth, each one pointed at the end.

She was in trouble and knew she would not hold out much longer. The treasure bag! Cana opened it and put her hand inside but all she pulled out was cheese — a block of it! *What evil god's trick is this?* she thought, but an idea took hold as the music began to drift across the water again.

Cana lay down in the boat, allowing the river to gently move the boat along. In her mouth was the pungent taste of the goat's cheese she was eating. The enchanting, inviting and fatal song of the merrows played out. But Cana could no longer hear it for two small chunks of cheese now plugged her ears.

The gentle bump on the bow told her she had made landfall. She was past the merrows. In front of her lay a length of desert wilderness lit by a much more intense brightness from above. What next? If this Suileach was as worrisome as Abcán described, she did not want to hang about, so she began to jog.

Halfway across the dusty plain, Cana felt a tremor underfoot. Stopping for a moment, she could feel it again. It was coming from below. She cupped her ear with her hand and brought her ear to the earth. She could feel that the tremors were increasing in intensity. As Cana knelt, she spotted what at first looked like a sandstorm. Her heart stood still. An enormous beast, as big and broad as the crown of an oak tree, was at the front of this dust cloud, hurtling towards her. She could see each of the thousand terrifying eyes of the Suileach.

With nowhere to run to and nowhere to hide, Cana froze. For a moment, an image of her life ending on the desert plain of the Otherworld struck her. 'Snap out of it!' she told herself. She knew her sword and shield were useless in the face of this monster, so once again she reached into the treasure bag. But once again what she took out confused her at first. It was a Celtic mirror, like the one Fionn had looked into the day of his inauguration as Fianna champion. On one side of the beautiful circular plate, ornate spirals danced, while on the other was the finest polished bronze. It reflected her angst-ridden face. *Reflection*, she thought.

The Suileach came crashing to a halt no more than a dozen feet from her. A cloud of dust shrouded it. When it cleared, the Suileach looked stunned, its mass of eyes blinking frenetically to rid themselves of particles of sand. But some of those eyes looked at her in anger — or in surprise. Not waiting to find out which, Cana flashed the mirror once again. The bright light from above reflected off it, blinding the hundreds of eyes that were trained on her.

The Suileach let out a piercing howl. And then it galloped away. Cana wiped away the dust that had settled on her and let out a deep breath. She turned towards the ridge of green in the distance and started walking.

The Suileach did not reappear, and before long Cana was striding down the path through the sparse forest. Around her were the great noble Irish trees: oak, pine, apple, ash, yew, holly and hazel. However, as soon as she saw it, she understood that no other tree ruled this woodland. Rowan trees should only grow some fifteen yards high, but from far away she could see this one – the Great Rowan Tree of Dubhros – was at least three times that. It was greater in size than any oak she had ever laid eyes on.

Despite, or perhaps because of, her encounters with death, Cana felt full of vigour. She had been made confident by her first two victories and the knowledge that no other warriors had reached this far. But time was ticking on. She decided not to creep, sneak or steal up to the tree but to walk straight up to it.

Searbhann was seated in the shade of the tree. At first, he appeared shocked at the arrival of this person, an uninvited stranger, brave and unabashed, who had walked right towards him. He stood up. Cana could now see why the forest was so thinly planted with trees. He was easily the height of the rowan, and the gaps between the other trees of this forested area were needed to allow him pass. She could also see why the other Tuatha Dé Danann feared him. He was far, far bigger than the giant that had visited Irish shores not that long before. And it wasn't just his size that was threatening. A thick iron belt looped around his body, from which hung an iron club with protruding nails as big as tree trunks. But there was one thing that Abcán had got wrong. Searbhann was no cyclops.

'Why are you here?' Searbhann demanded. 'Come to thieve the berries from this tree? Searbhann has been tasked by the Tuatha Dé Danann to guard these berries, and no one from this world or the one above will steal them from me.'

Cana stood her ground as Searbhann stomped forward. 'I did not come here to steal them. I came here to ask for them.'

Searbhann was silenced by her response.

'My friend is dying, and these berries will save him. I need them. He needs them. And that is why I have come to ask for them.'

'And what if I say no?'

'Then I will fight you for them.'

Searbhann laughed. 'You will not defeat me. I will crush you.'

'Probably,' Cana said, 'but it doesn't mean I won't try.'

Searbhann stared at her. Her answers surprised him, and he thought long and hard before speaking again. 'I will not just give them to you, but nor do I want to fight and kill you. Instead, give me something of equal value and they are yours.'

It was now Cana's turn to think. Searbhann retook his seat in front of the tree.

'You're not a cyclops,' Cana said, walking up to him.

'I can only see through one eye,' Searbhann answered.

'That doesn't make you a cyclops,' she said. 'It just means that you have one good eye. Do the berries not work?'

'For the Tuatha, the berries grant us eternal life but don't cure us of our ills.'

'What if I cured you?' Cana said.

Searbhann looked surprised. 'How?'

'My brother had a lazy eye when he was young. The older kids used to tease him over it. I did as well. We called him a cyclops until one day my mother came out and scared the other children away. She scolded me for leaving my brother to fend for himself. She then brought him inside and put a cloth around his good eye.'

'Leaving him blind?'

'No, leaving him almost blind, but I looked out for him. Over time, his lazy eye strengthened and soon both eyes were as good as each other.' Cana then opened her treasure bag and smiled. She began to pull out a cloth that seemed without end. When it was all out, she looked at Searbhann. 'If you let me, I'll strap your good eye for you.'

Searbhann bent down and soon Cana had covered his eye, the cloth tied tight. 'I won't be able to stay around to look out for you, though.'

The giant smiled. 'In case you have trouble seeing, I am as big as this tree. I think I'll be okay.' He stood up and somewhat clumsily picked three berries from the very top of the tree and gave them to Cana. She carefully placed them in a small pouch. Tucking it away, she turned to the giant.

'Thank you.'

'No. Thank *you*,' he replied.


Cana wasted no time returning along the path. The Suileach did not trouble her on her way back, and with enough cheese left over to drown out the songs of the merrows, she was soon rowing down to where Abcán had left her. When she reached the shoreline, night had not yet fallen. But there was no sign of Abcán or of his boat.

'Abcán?' she called as she walked along the shore. 'Abcán?' As before, the mist lay on the sea. 'Abc—' Cana abruptly stopped. On the beach stood five figures, with a dozen more behind. Many of them had animal-like facial features, which gave them all an air of the supernatural. Each was dressed in the most splendid of clothes — in every colour of the spectrum.

'You are the Tuatha Dé Danann,' Cana said.

'Yes. We are.' A man of great stature, clean-shaven, with vivid red hair, stepped forward. 'I am Bodb Derg, brother of Manannán Mac Lir, son of Dagda and the king of the Tuatha Dé Danann. And you are Cana.'

'Yes,' she replied.

'You shouldn't be here.'

'I was just leaving.'

'Not yet.'

'Why would you stop me?' Cana remained composed and determined. She had come this far and did not want to be stopped now.

'This is our world. Yours is above. My brother Manannán led us down here a long, long time ago when you took our lands. And now you come here uninvited?'

'First, we didn't take your lands. Your leaders refused to live in peace with us and then broke their word. Second, I am only down here because you still come to our lands.' Looking to the other Tuatha, she continued. 'Some of your children still live above among us, in peace.'

'That has stopped now,' said Bodb Derg. 'Under my reign, the Tuatha no longer disturb your lands.'

'They don't?' Cana said heatedly. 'Well, if the Tuatha don't come into our lands, how do you explain the attacks we've faced from dragons, sea serpents, wild stags and lake monsters? Why are we at war with a force that is spurred on by the Dealra Dubh?'

'We are not their friends and they do not speak for us,' Bodb Derg replied.

'But they are the Tuatha Dé Danann, are they not?'

Bodb Derg was silent.

'Try telling the families who've lost mothers and fathers, brothers and sisters, because their crops were destroyed, starving them of food, that these are different Tuatha. Or the loved ones of those who were killed defending their homes. Or someone whose loved one is now lying on his death bed because of the actions of a druid being led by your Tuatha.'

'She is right,' said a voice from behind Cana. It was Abcán, bringing his boat to shore. 'This woman has done you no harm. It is we who should send an apology back with her. Now leave her be and let me return her to her people.'

No one said another word. Not as Cana boarded the boat. Not when Abcán rowed away from shore. And not when they entered the mists once more. Indeed, they both travelled in silence for some time before Cana spoke.

'You know, you sound a lot like Finnegas?'

Abcán gave a sad smile. 'Do I?'

'Yes, you do. You also look a little like him too. Younger, of course.'

At this, she noticed a tear had come to Abcán's eye, but he rubbed it away quickly.

'I hope I didn't insult you,' she added, trying to make light of what she had said.

But Abcán just smiled. 'It's not an insult to be compared with your grandson.'

'What? But he is older than you!' Cana said.

'Time moves much slower here in our world,' he replied. He opened his mouth to speak again but stopped, his attention now ahead of him. 'We're here.'

Cana sat up and looked around. They had cleared the mists. She could see Cnes sitting on the riverbank. Cana hopped from the boat to shore and triumphantly held out the small pouch with the berries. She was greeted with a warm embrace and what also looked like tears.

'You're crying! You didn't think I'd make it back?' Cana laughed.

'I had begun to lose hope.'

'It hasn't been a day, and you gave up on me?'

'A day? You have been gone five!'

'You're lying!' Cana looked back to Abcán, who was already rowing into the mist. She could see his knowing smile, and his words 'time moves much slower here in our world' rang in her ears. 'We must have very little time left!'

'A day — if we're not already too late,' Cnes answered.

Rarely had horses covered ground as fast as those of Cana and Cnes, who arrived back at Tara just before sundown. Fionn's breathing was fading. An hour later,

Eitne had prepared a paste from the berries and applied it to his festering wound.

'What now?' Cana asked, her body suddenly exhausted.

'We wait and see if he makes it through the night.'


'Cana. Cana! Oh, Canaaa?'

Cana awoke with a start, grabbing her sword and skene dagger before her eyes were even open.

'Woah! Mind the pointy end!' Cnes shouted. 'Do you want him at death's door again?'

Looking at her, as healthy and lively as he had been the day she'd met him, was Fionn. He was a few years older now, with a few more scars to show for it — but it was Fionn!

'You're alive!' she shouted, dropping her weapons and hugging him. Letting go and stepping back from him to take it all in, she could barely contain her glee. 'Wow! Last night you ... you were —'

'Dying, I know. Eitne told me what you did to save me. Thank you.'

'You'd have done the same. I thought the berries would work but didn't expect that you'd look so ...?'

'Alive?' Fionn suggested.

'Yes, alive.' Cana laughed 'And the wound?'

'Better,' he said. Holding up his tunic, he revealed where the spear had pierced him, which was now infection-free and almost healed.

'The berries?'

'Yes, the berries,' answered Eitne, who was now standing nearby.

Cana looked at Fionn and felt a wave of happiness and relief. But then she thought of someone else. 'Sadb?'

'Eitne told me when I woke,' said Fionn.

'I'm sorry.'

'Eitne said that when you reached the beach there was no sign of her?'

'None,' Cana replied. 'She may have been taken away on Tadg's boat. It was already far out to sea, but no one knows for sure.'

'Tadg does,' Fionn said, looking forlornly east.

'Here, in case I forget,' Cana said, offering his treasure bag back to him. 'It got me out of several tight spots.'

'Then keep it. A thank-you for saving my life,' he said. 'Maybe it will get you out of several more.'

In the Royal Hall, Art was reading a message that Crimmal had just handed him from a messenger bird. It was from Ernamis, who was now at sea, looking for signs of an approaching enemy fleet. The message was not good, and after reading it, Art looked at Crimmal, who nodded knowingly. 'They're coming,' said Art. 'Send for Fionn.'

# THE BATTLE OF VENTRY

'Welcome aboard, little brother.' Goll held out his hand for his younger sibling Conan to grab and jump up on deck. 'Impressive fleet, isn't it?'

Conan nodded. Around them were some forty ships with about two thousand men. Goll had just led twenty of these from the Isle of Manau to where his brother Conan had anchored another twenty ships along the Isle of Mona, just off the coast of Cymru, eighty miles east of Ireland. Aboard them were some of the fiercest mercenary warriors – not just of those lands, but also of Scotland, Albion, Gaul and Lochlann.

'How was your trip out?' Goll asked.

'Some quarrelling between the Brigantes and the Coritanians but otherwise fine. The seas have been kind.'

'The seas will continue to be kind.' Goll smiled malevolently. He looked at Tadg, who was standing at the bow of the ship.

'Are you sure that what we are doing is right?' Conan asked.

Goll turned around in surprise. 'What do you mean? We're taking back what is ours, what is our family's birthright.'

'Our birthright is as heads of the Fianna, not High Kings of Ireland. But I'm not asking about that, I'm asking about him — the Dark Druid. Are we right to fight alongside him? He does not serve us. He serves the Dealra Dubh.'

'I'm well aware of who he serves. But for the time being we both have a common enemy — Fionn Mac Cumhaill of Clan Bascna — and that is all that matters. Have you forgotten about your foster-sister, Berrach?'

Conan looked down at the deck.

'Maybe you were too young, but I was not, and I will never forget. Now, let's set sail. We have a long voyage ahead.'

As the anchor was raised a favourable breeze picked up. Goll looked into the distance. In the wind he could hear his foster-sister calling.

'Little brother? Where have you gone?'

Goll smiled as he peered out from the thicket of young buckthorns he had hidden behind. He was not known as Goll back then, though. He still had sight in both eyes. It was his birth name, Áed, that his foster-sister, Berrach Brecc, was calling out as she tried to find him.

'Come on, Áed,' she called again, becoming irritated by his hide-and-seek antics. 'Our parents will be waiting, and I'll get into trouble.'

On hearing his parents mentioned, Goll's smile disappeared. He didn't want his sister, some twelve years older than him, getting into trouble. Not with their parents. His father, Morna, was a difficult man who never acted fairly and cursed the man who acted fairly towards him. Goll's mother, Ailill, had been a fierce fighter who punished the smallest mistake with a slap or thump. Indeed, love and care were foreign to both his parents. It had been Berrach who had nurtured any happiness in him, and he idolised his big sister for that.

From the undergrowth, Goll watched as Berrach became increasingly frustrated. Suddenly her attention was drawn elsewhere. He could hear the sound of hooves approaching. Goll hid and watched. A pony appeared. It was Trénmor, the champion of the Fianna, who had taken his father's title by defeating him in a wrestling bout. He was speaking to Berrach now. She looked scared and uncertain. She looked around for Goll. He thought she called his name. He had wanted to step forward, but something stopped him. Maybe he was scared too. A moment later, she was sitting behind Trénmor, now galloping away.

That night, he remembered the fury in his parents' voices. Then the noise of Morna's men, who came to their house. There were angry shouts and cheers, curses and threats. When he awoke the next morning, something was still wrong. He felt scared again. Something bad had happened during the night. He had lost something he could not get back. When he saw Berrach's body brought home that afternoon, he understood that loss, and from his parent's talk, he was in no doubt who was responsible for the death of his foster-sister. It was Clan Bascna's fault, and the only thing that could fill the gap that Berrach's death left in his heart was hate towards Clan Bascna and all who carried that name.

Eighty miles west of Goll's fleet, on a teardrop-shaped peninsula known as Eadar's Peak, just north of what one day would be known as Dublin, Fionn, Crimmal and Connla stood beside each other. They were looking out to sea, the hounds Conbec and Cuaird beside them.

'Still no sign.'

'No,' Crimmal answered solemnly.

'They may not come, you know,' said Connla.

'They will,' Fionn replied. 'Ernamis's message was clear: twenty ships at Cymru, fully laden with warriors and soldiers, and another twenty on their way down to meet them from the Isle of Manau. Goll's wait is over.'

Connla nodded. 'Did you hear what the Chief Druid said last night, about the feast of Lughnasa that is fast approaching?'

'Yes,' said Fionn.

'Why Lughnasa?'

'The Chief Druid believes that during these annual Celtic feasts the powers of Otherworldly forces are at their zenith. And it will be on that day that the forces of the Dealra Dubh will pour forth from Rathcroghan. That is why Tadg returned to Rathcroghan to open it, and it is why I believe he will return there to unite these evil forces of the Dealra Dubh with Goll's forces from overseas. That is why we have sent Cana, Diorraing, Ossnat and Covey with a battalion of soldiers and several hounds there to protect it. The High Druid has also accompanied them there to try to seal it shut.'

'And Tadg will have to come through us if he wants to get to Rathcroghan,' said Crimmal. 'Every major invasion I can recall has happened on the beaches below us, where boats are able to land easily. However, if Goll,

Tadg and their army try a beach elsewhere, we have warriors and soldiers stationed up and down this coast.'

Connla bade them goodbye and returned to his hounds to make sure they too were ready. As he departed, a messenger ran past him and up to Fionn. 'News, my captain.'

'What is it?' Fionn asked.

'More word from the sea — from the ship of Ernamis.'

Fionn took the message and read it: '"A fleet of forty ships sailing directly south. A strong wind pushing them on. Will continue pursuit."'

'Why south?' he said to Crimmal. He turned back to the messenger. 'Inform the High King of this. Then send word to our coastal defences further south, instructing them to be on high alert.'

Fionn, Crimmal and Art looked at the map of the country, trying to work out where Goll's army and Tadg would come ashore.

'They've chosen not to meet us at full strength along our eastern coast. Instead, they're heading south, believing us to be more vulnerable there,' Fionn said.

'And no ships were spotted breaking away?' Art asked.

'No, none.'

'That doesn't make sense. Tadg will be as far from Rathcroghan as you can get.'

'I don't understand it either,' Fionn said. 'But we need to start moving our forces now, ready for wherever they land.'

'That wind hasn't let up since we pulled anchor yesterday,' Conan said to Goll, who, in the first light of morning, was admiring a map that showed his old homeland.

'Nor will it until we arrive — our crew-mate will ensure that,' he said, looking over to Tadg.

'And how long will that be?' Conan asked.

Goll looked to his map and at a long toe of land that extended from Ireland's south-west into the great ocean. 'To the beach of Ventry, where most of us will land, it will take another day. By the time Fionn and his Fianna know what has happened, we will have made our way through the peninsula into open country and be waiting for him. Meanwhile, Tadg will continue up the Shannon with two boats towards the sidhe of Rathcroghan.'

'Up the River Shannon? How is that possible?' Conan asked, astounded.

'The same way it is possible to have fair winds from Cymru to Kerry, brother. Don't you see the magical power that this druid brings us? In a few days it will be Lughnasa, and a full moon too. Tadg will return to Rathcroghan and meet the Dealra Dubh and his forces. They will come down on the Fianna from the north, and we will come up at the Fianna from below, and we will snap their backs like dried hazel sticks — and this island will be ours.'

While Goll sailed on, a badly wounded Ernamis was readying one final messenger bird. In the darkness of night she had used all her seafaring skills to chase down and pick off a lagging ship from the enemy fleet. On boarding it, there had been a crashing, furious and bloody battle. Ernamis and her soldiers were outnumbered against a well-armed group of Parisi mercenaries from northern Gaul. But she had drawn on the spirit of her late sister Échna and had fought with frenzied intensity, winning a battle she had no right to. In the cold, hard light of day, the cost of combat became clear. Many of her fellow fighters lay dead or grievously wounded. But they had succeeded and got what they had come for. In the dying breath of a foreign mercenary she was given a name. Ventry Beach. Goll's fleet were to land at Ventry Beach.

'Checkmate.'

'Again?'

'Yes,' Lugach said, grinning broadly at Donn. He had just won his third straight game of brandubh. 'Although, when I moved forward earlier with my queen and you clapped your hands, I was sure I had played myself into trouble.'

'Yes, you were lucky. I had you but then I got distracted and let my advantage slip.' Donn had, of course, not let his advantage slip. When it came to games of strategy and thought, Lugach was always a few steps ahead, though Donn would never admit it. Instead, his favourite tactic was to let on he knew what he was doing and pretend he was never far from winning the game himself.

The pair were stationed at the south-east corner of Fionn's defences, along with Fiacha. A little further north were Cnes, Iollan and Cailte with their battalion of soldiers, and this continued with other Fianna warriors manning forts and defences the whole way up the eastern shores as far as Ulster.

'One more game, my friend, before we begin our watch?' Lugach asked, but before Donn could answer the thunderous sound of the Barr Buadh cut in, soon echoed to their north. The Barr Buadh was a horn the druids had made to replace the Dord Fiann, many of which had been lost in the blaze of Tara. Its cry travelled further than the Dord and it was used as a call to arms that every Fianna answered with a shout, each warrior vying to be first.

'The enemy fleet?' Donn shouted to Lugach as they both ran to where Fiacha, painted in the blue of the woad plant, was sounding the instrument. But the seas were empty.

'What is it?' Lugach asked.

'Another message,' replied Fiacha.

'From Fionn?'

'No, from Ernamis aboard her ship. She knows where Goll and his fleet are landing. Ventry Beach.'

'Ventry Beach?' said Donn. 'But that's all the way down in ...'

'Kerry,' said Fiacha, 'which is many miles away and why we need to get moving immediately. I have already sent messenger birds with this news to Fionn and the rest of our army further north. Those of us with horses and hounds will gallop ahead. Our foot soldiers will need to quick-march their way as fast they can. Ventry Beach is as safe a landing point as Goll could choose, entirely unprotected and far from our forces. But it is at the edge of a peninsula. Goll will try and get his army off it and into open land as quickly as possible. If we can get across in time and gather whatever fighting men and women are left in these areas, we might be able to hold them until reinforcements and our foot soldiers arrive. How Ernamis has got hold of this information I don't know, but she has bought us some precious time that we must not waste.'

All day and through the night, the trio of warriors had not stopped. They had pushed ahead to Ventry Beach, where they met the elderly Chief Anlon, who still ruled this fiefdom of Kerry. Together, they now lay on their bellies on a bluff above the sands, looking down.

'In all your years, Fiacha, have you ever had to defend the Fianna from a force like this?' Lugach asked.

'Never,' said Fiacha.

On the long horseshoe of flat strand that was the beach at Ventry, men of every description were organising along its golden sands. From lands overseas, soldiers had come with their banners of various colours — blue, green, red and white — containing images of yew-tree, oak, mountain ash, stag, sword, battle-axe, bagpipes and horn. In the bay, well protected from the ocean's waves, nearly forty ships — thirty-seven to be exact — had dropped anchor. And it was this number that was the topic of conversation between Goll and Conan.

'Where are the Parisis?' Goll asked angrily. 'There should be thirty-eight ships.'

'I don't know,' replied Conan. 'They're not known for their seafaring and were lagging behind us as we travelled down the eastern coast.'

Goll growled but could do little. 'It's fifty mercenaries. We still have nearly two thousand here. Get the chiefs of these groups ready and we'll move inland within the hour.'

High above, Donn, Lugach, Fiacha and Chief Anlon were considering their plans, when the familiar and welcome sight of Cnes, Cailte and Iollan appeared.

'What have we missed so far?' asked Iollan, smiling as he crept up beside them.

'Oh, you know,' Donn replied, 'two thousand foreign fighters, mercenaries, a Silurian cavalry and Mac Morna men settling down for a big day out at the beach. We're hoping they'll stick to making sand-forts and some paddling before returning home.'

'Presuming they don't,' said Lugach, 'how long before we can expect reinforcements?'

'It could be a few hours before the first of our foot soldiers make it here,' said Cnes. 'And Fionn, Crimmal and the main body of Fianna warriors were about two hours north of us at Eadar's Peak.'

'So, what do we do in the meantime?'

'Well, we won't fight them on the beach,' said Fiacha. 'Eight of us against some two thousand are not great odds. We need to retreat to where we can narrow their point of attack.'

'Then we'll need to go to the River of Shadows,' said Chief Anlon, 'where the watercourse spills down from the mountains and heads out to sea. It's the closest thing we have to a bottle-neck on the southern route off this peninsula.'

'Is that the only way off?' Cnes asked.

'No, there is one other route. Up there.' Chief Anlon nodded towards the mountains to their north. 'A mountain pass that cuts through those peaks, known as the Bearna Baoil. At its narrowest only one person can pass through.'

Quickly the Fianna came to a decision. Fiacha and Cnes would take six of Chief Anlon's best soldiers and hold the pass, while the rest would take the southern route.

When Lugach, Donn, Iollan, Cailte and Chief Anlon arrived at the river, they were met by Chief Rian and Chief Cearbhall from the other fiefdoms of Kerry further south. With them were more soldiers, some very young and others quite old. However, they soon realised that, even with the more than one hundred soldiers they now had, it was still too wide and would be impossible to defend.

'We need more soldiers,' Cailte said.

'We need more time,' Lugach replied. 'That will bring us more soldiers.'

'But how do we get it?'

'Maybe we could put a brave face on?' said Donn.

'What?' said Lugach.

'Put on a brave face. It's what I do in brandubh. I always pretend I'm in a stronger position than I really am — especially when I play you, my friend. I look confident and you think I've set a trap. It slows you down, as you begin thinking about how I might beat you, when in fact, all I'm doing is wondering how long will it take me to lose!'

Lugach smiled as his friend's words gave him an idea.

Goll was standing at the front of his men. Already, almost half of his force was moving north to leave the peninsula via the Bearna Baoil. He was taking the other half along its southern coastline. However, he had brought the army to a stop.

'What's wrong?' Conan asked.

'There,' Goll said, pointing to Cailte, who was sitting and singing without a care on a small ridge some hundred yards away.

'Who is it?' Conan asked.

'I don't know, but from his clothes he is a Fianna warrior.'

'Well, let's go and kill him then,' Conan replied impatiently.

'I want to, but I don't understand what a Fianna warrior is doing here all alone. They should be on the other side of this island. Since we've arrived, we haven't met one inhabitant. Every hamlet and village is empty and now this Fianna warrior is just sitting there singing.'

'Do you think it's a trap?'

'Yes.'

'Then what do we do?'

'I don't know.'

Though Cailte may have looked relaxed, he was anything but. He knew that the eyes of a thousand warriors and mercenaries were on him. However, Lugach and Donn's plan was working so far. His solo presence had spooked Goll and, fearing a trap, he had yet to move forward. Not too far behind Cailte was the River of Shadows, though it was quickly becoming just a stream. Donn had outperformed himself with another idea, recalling the story Eitne had told him of the giant otter her group had encountered at Lough Ree. This had fostered an idea to dam the river high up in the hills, which at that very moment Iollan and some local soldiers were working on.

Further up in the mountains another stream was flowing. Except this one was slowly running upwards and was made of men. Enemy warriors and mercenaries were approaching and expecting to travel through the Bearna Baoil. But two Fianna warriors and a half-dozen local soldiers had backed themselves into the narrowest of mountain passes to plug the enemy's path forward. Where they stood, the mountain rose in sheer cliffs to their left, while to their right the ground fell away to a deep, dark fall that could only end in death.

It was here that the Fianna made their first stand.

As fighting broke out high above, down below Goll had grown restless, as he had allowed the hours to tick by in indecision. Eventually, as the sun reached its peak, he decided he could not wait any longer.

'Send for the Silurians and their horses,' he ordered Conan.

Cailte saw movement and the readying of horses. There was going to be a cavalry charge, one which he had no interest in meeting on his own. He quickly jumped down and retreated over the river to where Donn, Lugach and the local chiefs now waited.

'Goll, look!' Conan pointed to the spot where Cailte had been sitting, which was now empty.

Goll cursed, realising that he had been tricked, and with a roar ordered the Silurian cavalry to begin the attack.

'Closer, closer, closer,' Lugach was whispering to himself as the Silurian cavalry began to increase speed changing up from a gallop to a charge, the forces of Goll following close behind. The very sight of them, being among the most skilled and feared horsemen in Cymru, could strike fear into the hearts of the bravest of men. But Lugach held his nerve and waited. 'Closer, closer, closer, NOW!'

Immediately the call of a Barr Buadh was sounded and Iollan heard the signal to break down what he had built up, collapsing the dam and releasing a flood.

Suddenly, the trembling of the ground coming from the cavalry, almost upon them, was replaced by heavier rumblings high up in the hills — a noise that grew in intensity until the white froth of rushing water could be seen. And seen too late by the oncoming Silurians, their horses and many of the warriors who were following them. *Crash* went the water with a deafening roar as the vast torrent swept the first waves of the enemy forces away and threw the rest of Goll's army back, to retreat in disarray.

The sound of the Barr Buadh reached the mountain pass as Fiacha was continuing to hold the Bearna Baoil.

Fiacha, Cnes and the others had all taken turns to defend this narrow path. Already they had lost half their number, as four local warriors had been struck down. However, far more of the enemy had been defeated and they had held the path. Of those who fought it was Fiacha who had taken most turns defending the pass, dispatching enemy challenger after challenger. But he had not come through these fights unscathed and was already weakened by the time he met an enormous and infamous Lochlann warrior by the name of Egil Ironblood. Towering over Fiacha, Egil, with a great long sword and small round wooden shield, drove at him. It was a fierce scuffle and one where Egil's fierce tattooed face roared and shouted at Fiacha's woad-covered face, which bellowed back. But in the end, Fiacha's fatigue from previous fights was too much.

Cnes could only watch as one of the Fianna's most loyal servants fell in front of her. But she did not cry out. Instead, carrying two spears in her hands, she marched forward with no great fear of the warrior before her and little for who was behind him. Despite her own wounds, she met Egil with deathly skill and speed, fatally wounding him with three savage thrusts that knocked him from the narrow path, sending him to his end far below. She then took Fiacha's place and continued to hold firm.

Back down below, Lugach could see Goll's army had regathered and was approaching once again. Caledonians from Scotland with their sharp, pointed turquoise javelins; the Unelli from Gaul with their great broad, grey spears; northern Lochlann invaders identifiable by their dark purple shields; and their southern lowland neighbours who were known for their tall gold-socketed spears and white-painted shoulders. This time there would be no ruse, no trap. This time they would be outnumbered.

The Fianna force let loose their arrows, cast their darts, their javelins and finally their slings. With each weapon, a line of enemy soldiers was struck and sank down, but still they kept coming. Surely this was the end.

But then came the sound of the Barr Buadh once more — this time from behind their lines. And then in the distance barking, growing louder. Suddenly a pack of wolfhounds burst past them, tearing into the oncoming enemy. Lugach could then hear the eternally angry voice of Sárait beside him, annoyed, it seemed, that the battle had begun without her. And then his champion, Fionn, with Conbec alongside, appeared. The Barr Buadh was sounded again, but instead of a wave of water crashing into Goll and his men, it was now Fionn and a wave of Fianna warriors and the quick-marching army of reinforcements.

High above, uncertainty spread among the enemy ranks as word rose up of Goll's forces being driven back to Ventry Beach. Fear of being cut off by an advancing Fianna force spread, and soon the enemy and mercenary forces were also retreating down the slopes, leaving a shattered, spent and blood-soaked Cnes to collapse on the ground in relief.

If it had only been foreign soldiers they were facing, the now Fionn-led Fianna and the army of Irish soldiers inspired by the High King of Ireland that had also arrived to the fray would doubtless have won. However, Goll's forces contained their own legendary warriors, who were a match for Fionn's. As a result, no sooner had Fionn managed to push Goll's army back to the beach than an enemy fight-back began. And this back and forth continued throughout the night until exhaustion pulled the forces away from each other.

Word came to Goll the next morning — a request and an invitation. 'What are they, brother?' he asked Conan.

'The first is from the High King, Art, requesting that this morning the bodies of the fallen be collected so they can be given funeral rites.'

'I accept. Many of our kinsmen lie out there. It is right that we take them back. And the invitation?'

'From Fionn Mac Cumhaill. He asks that this war is ended by single combat with the champions of both forces. If you accept, he asks you to name the weapon you wish to fight with.'

Goll looked out from his tent, pitched beside the marram-covered dunes of Ventry. The tide had been low during the night and had not yet washed the blood off the beach. He had lived for over fifty years and could not remember a day of carnage like the one he had just witnessed. 'Tell him I accept. And tell him I choose the battle-axe.'

In the royal tent, news of the terrible losses that the Fianna and their forces had sustained was being relayed. No sooner had Crimmal completed the list of known dead than his attention was drawn to a runner who had just arrived.

'A reply from Goll?' the High King asked.

'Yes,' the runner answered. 'He consents to an exchange of bodies.' Then looking to Fionn, he added, 'And he would like to end this. This afternoon. With battle-axes.'

'Fionn? Are you here?'

'Crimmal? Come in. I'm just getting ready.'

'Do you need a hand?'

'No. I'm fine, thanks.' Fionn was finishing his strapping for battle, determined to remain unburdened by heavy armour. Goll was bigger and stronger than him, and no type of armour would shield him from a direct blow of his battle-axe, so it was better to stay light and mobile.

'How are you feeling?'

'A little nervous.' Then, looking at Conbec, who lay at the entrance to the tent looking forlorn, as if sensing that he would not accompany his master, Fionn added, 'I think we are both nervous. Not because of what might happen to me, but because of what might happen to the country if I lose.'

'Don't be.' Crimmal tried to reassure him.

'Can I ask you something, uncle?'

'Go ahead.'

'I never thought to ask before, but why does Goll hate me with such passion?'

'He doesn't. He just hates our family, Clan Bascna. He thinks we are responsible for the death of his foster sister when he was a child.'

'And were we?'

'No, not unless loving someone is a crime. She and your grandfather Trénmor fell in love. It was after your grandmother — my mother — had died. And Cumhall and I were still very small. They escaped to get married and Goll's family wouldn't accept it. In the battle that followed, she was killed by a stray arrow. No one knows from whose bow it came. But they have never forgiven us — he has never forgiven us.'

'Is that why the High King barred Fianna warriors from marrying for a time?'

'Yes.'

After a pause, Fionn said, 'But that was such a long time ago.'

'I know,' Crimmal replied. 'That's what allowing hate and anger to grow and fester in your heart can do to you.'

At the very moment Crimmal and Fionn were talking, Cana and Caicer were also in conversation deep in the sidhe of Rathcroghan.

'I'm afraid it's proving harder to seal than I thought.'

'Why?'

'I'm not sure. It could be a stronger force of magic than I can produce. Or it might just be that I have yet to find the right spell. I will continue looking.'

Cana looked concerned. Holding a flaming torch to guide her way, she had helped lead Caicer into the depths of the sidhe, walking first down a darkening passageway, the temperature dropping with each step. They had then arrived at where a gargantuan hunk of rock had been slid aside and a portal had been opened. Through this, on the other side, the cave widened and the temperature warmed. Finally, at the other side of it was a stone-arched bridge that spanned a great crevice, too wide to jump across and too dark to see how far it plunged.

Pointing into the dark distance across the bridge, Caicer had explained that it was from there that the forces of the Dealra Dubh would arrive with the setting of the sun outside and that he needed to destroy this bridge to the Otherworld and seal the portal shut.

'Sunset is not far away,' Cana said now. 'Will you have enough time?'

'I will do my best.'

In the distance, the echo of a shout reached them. Cana wished the Chief Druid well and took off for the entrance where Diorraing, Ossnat, Covey and some thirty soldiers were keeping guard.

'What is it?' Cana said as she emerged from the sidhe.

'There.' Diorraing pointed to the enemy soldiers fast approaching. 'As many as fifty, I reckon. And look closely at the figure who leads them.'

Cana's eyes readjusted to the daylight and, as they did, the hunched, bearded, unmistakable figure of Tadg could be seen. 'Right. Everyone, you know your positions.'

The afternoon sun had begun to cloud over. On the beach stood Goll, defiant, rebellious, unwavering. Facing him, stood Fionn. Around them in broad semi-circles were their forces. Many had spent the morning collecting the bodies of their friends and fellow fighters.

'Fionn Mac Cumhaill of Clan Bascna, you began all this when you took the captaincy of the Fianna from me, and your clan began it many moons before that when they killed my sister, Berrach Brecc. Today I will have my revenge.'

'You may try, Áed "Goll" Mac Morna, but before you do, I did take the captaincy of the Fianna from you, as was my right. But my family did not kill your sister. Yours did. And she would have been a grandparent to me had they let her and Trénmor be. But they did not. Nor did you leave my parents be. So, one of us will have their revenge today.'

'*Grrrr!*' Goll charged at Fionn with a speed that belied his years. His battle-axe, though it was the size of Fionn from toe to chin, was held in just one hand and he swung it with ease, as one would a twig. Fionn, surprised by the sudden charge, managed to just about avoid his first set of blows before bringing his own battle-axe down with force, a blow that Goll parried away. Goll advanced again, this time more focused. Once again, he pushed Fionn back, making him parry and evade, parry and evade. Occasionally, Fionn got his own strikes in, but Goll's skill with the battle-axe easily equalled his own.

Time passed and the weight of the axe began to slow Fionn. Having dodged another swing of Goll's axe, Fionn swung his own, only for it to be deflected down into the sand, where it lodged. It was a split-second but that was all Goll needed to crash down his own blow. Fionn eluded it by a hair's breadth. But Goll's axe smashed Fionn's to smithereens. Fionn was now without a weapon, except for a dagger that all soldiers could carry in such battles. Goll saw this and smiled. He knew victory was within reach.

Fionn knew it too. The shadow cast from the battle-axe approached him. But then, an idea. 'The shadow.' Looking up, he could see that the late-afternoon clouds had cleared and he remembered Cana's stories from beneath. Sidestepping another swing, his foot struck the head of his broken battle-axe lying in the sand.

Goll saw him pick it up and laughed. 'Are you going to throw that at me?'

But as he bore down on Fionn for another blow, Fionn caught the bright August sunlight off the axe-head's metal face. Shining it at Goll, he blinded him. It lasted a moment but was enough to allow Fionn to roll, dodge and stab — a piercing strike in Goll's side.

'Ah!' he roared. 'What sort of deception is this?'

'None — I used the battle-axe. I just didn't throw it at you.'

Goll roared again and ran at Fionn, who again eluded him. And again. And again. Soon Goll's attacks grew infrequent. Not because of fatigue but because Fionn had caught him well. He had been cut deep and the loss of blood robbed him of his strength. Then Goll was on his knees, the battle-axe lying alone on the sand.

'It's over,' Fionn said, squatting down beside Goll, who nodded. 'We have great healers — let me send for one. That wound is serious, but you need not die.'

Goll turned his head to Fionn and, for the first time in a long time, his face was not filled with fury. 'Let my anger die with me on this beach. It has lived with me for too long.'

Fionn nodded. 'I will honour my promise and your people will be allowed to leave.'

'My brother, Conan?'

'He will not be harmed.'

It was Goll's turn to nod. 'I'm sorry, though.'

'Why?' Fionn asked.

Goll groaned before again looking at Fionn. 'Your island is still not safe.'

Fionn took a moment before it sank in. 'Rathcroghan? Tadg?'

Goll nodded once more and then passed from this world.


Thwing! Thwing!

Diorraing could hear the fletching of Ossnat's arrows rhythmically take off, with the sound of a shout or roar an instant later as they met their mark. She could let three go before he even had one shot off.

'Don't worry, my love,' Ossnat said, sensing Diorraing's growing frustration. 'This is where I come into my own. Your strength will soon be needed if these enemy soldiers breach our defences.'

And she was right. Despite the best efforts of those on the hill of Rathcroghan, Tadg's forces, which outnumbered those defending by about two to one, broke through on the hill's northern slope as they shifted all their energy and numbers to that side.

'Fasten up our northern flanks,' Cana shouted, directing their numbers across to try and repel those who had broken through. In the hand-to-hand and forceful combat that followed it was perhaps only due to Diorraing's great strength and the ferocity with which their wolfhounds attacked that the enemy was finally beaten and driven back. However, any relief was short-lived when Cana returned to the sidhe's entrance where Covey lay bleeding. 'What happened?'

'I'm sorry,' Covey said, grimacing in pain. 'I was guarding the sidhe as you'd instructed when I saw you draw near. I was sure of it. But when you were within arm's length, I realised I was wrong. But it was too late. I had been stabbed, and holding the dagger was Tadg, not you.'

Cana could see that, though he was wounded, the bleeding had already been staunched and bandaged.

'Créde,' he said. 'She has followed him inside.'

'Don't speak, save your energy.' Cana then turned to the others. 'Tadg. He must have concentrated his forces to our northern flank to allow him sneak past.' She then instructed one of her lieutenants to shore up their defences, treat the injured and ready themselves for combat if what was left of the enemy returned. She turned then to Ossnat and Diorraing. 'Grab a pair of torches and come with me.'

Caicer heard the steps approaching before he saw Cana's face appear.

'How are you doing?' she said.

'Still nothing,' Caicer replied. 'I fear it is useless, that I do not have the strength or the tools to close it.'

'Maybe you could use this?' Cana said, smiling and holding out the Great Book of Moytura.

'H-how on earth did you get that?' Caicer asked, dumbfounded.

'With this.'

Cana held out the Bóinne Mace Head. None of it made sense — but then it all did. He looked at Cana's face, and even in the gloom of the cave he could see that it was not her eyes he was looking at, but Tadg's. A phosphorescent blast of light lit up the cavern as Tadg struck Caicer with his staff, sending him crashing against the wall of the sidhe. Caicer only had time to look back up and see the whole figure of Tadg, now in his original form, before he was struck again and everything went black.

As Caicer slumped to the floor, Tadg heard footsteps. 'And who are you?' he asked, turning to meet the female figure who had arrived.

'Créde,' she answered slowly, walking towards him. 'You were responsible for the death of my love, Cál Crodae.'

'The warrior on the beach. With the spear?' Tadg smiled cruelly.

'Yes.'

'And what are you going to do about it? Where are your weapons?'

'I am a healer. We don't carry weapons.'

Cana, Ossnat and Diorraing then also entered the inner hall.

'Ah ... of course, like Fionn's love, Sadb. She was also a healer. Though she bit me.'

'Yes, the animal spirit in her.'

'Indeed, the animal spirit. Do you know the interesting thing about healers?' Tadg asked, a malevolent quality in his eyes. 'They are more vulnerable to magic than other humans. They can be turned into their other selves quite easily, into that part of them which is Tuatha.'

'I know,' Créde said defiantly, running towards Tadg, who smiled and drew his staff upwards before striking a blast of unnatural light against her, stopping her in her tracks. Then raising the Bóinne Mace Head once more aloft, he used an incantation to cast a spell on her.

In unison, Cana, Diorraing and Ossnat attacked, but Tadg stopped them too, throwing them back violently against the wall behind.

'Ha!' he cackled. 'Foolish Fianna warriors who think they can use strength to defeat me: Tadg, servant of the Dealra Dubh, who – Arrgghhh!'

From her prone position, Cana saw Tadg being slapped with such might that his staff and sacred text burst from his grip and he was sent to the floor with violent force. Where he had stood, a huge brown bear – an animal that hadn't been seen in these parts for more than a generation – had emerged. And a moment later it was atop him. '*No!*' he cried with blood-curdling intensity. 'This cannot be! What have you become! Arrgghhh!'

Tadg was being held in the bear's jaws. A vice-like grip – ferocious, brutal, vicious. The Dark Druid's screams heightened, filling every inch of the cavern, as he was shaken like a sodden rag, side to side, up and down, against the ground with deadening thuds, until there was silence. The bear opened its jaws and

Tadg's body dropped to the floor. Then a great big paw struck it and it disappeared into the dark abyss. Gone. For ever.

The bear passed Cana and Diorraing slowly picking themselves off the floor. Before it left, it stopped and looked back at them. While it was undoubtedly an animal, Cana recognised its eyes. 'Créde?' she mouthed softly.

And the bear appeared to dip its head before disappearing.

'Urrggh!'

'Chief Druid!' Cana ran over to Caicer, who was beginning to regain consciousness.

'Tadg?'

'Dead.'

'What? How?'

'Créde, though not Créde. I'll explain later, but let's get you up now. We still need to seal this sidhe shut.'

'And it doesn't look like we have much time.' Diorraing pointed across the bridge and further into the cave, where a light was beginning to grow.

'They're coming,' Caicer muttered. 'We need to destroy this bridge.' However, no sooner had he picked up the Bóinne Mace Head and the Great Book of Moytura than the first force of evil bounded into view: a wolf, its jaws aflame.

'Watch out!' cried Cana as she spun and swung her sword, striking down the creature as it crossed the bridge towards them. 'Quick — return to the outer hall and close the sidhe door from there. I will hold what comes at us. Hurry!'

'Let me stay,' Diorraing shouted, but Cana shook her head before pointing to Ossnat, who had yet to stand from Tadg's blow and was in considerable distress.

'I can't carry her and the druid will need some help. Go! Now! *Go!*'

Another wolf, another strike, and the enchanted beast fell howling into the chasm below. The light from beyond intensified and so too did the noise. Horses. By instinct Cana knew what it was: the phantom cavalry of the sidhe. She had heard stories of them as a child, nine undead warriors sworn to lay waste to the world above. In one hand she held her sword, in the other a shield. She could feel every contour of their handles. She noticed her hands were dry. She was conscious of every sensation around her and then, for a moment, was away with Cnes, Iollan and Fionn, laughing, talking, joking. And then she was back, and in the far distance she could see the headless riders approach. She then felt something else. A strap around her neck. The treasure bag. Created to help keep a hero of men and women safe from the threat of an evil Tuatha. How would it work against the threat of nine evil Tuatha and all that lay behind them? She put her hand into the bag and smiled.

'Here?' Fionn asked.

'Yes.' The Chief Druid nodded. Beside him stood Diorraing, with Ossnat nearby, her broken leg now strapped.

'And no sound has been heard for more than a day?'

'None.'

Fionn stroked his hand along the flat granite surface of the colossal rock and looked to the High King, who nodded.

'Open it, Chief Druid,' commanded Art. 'And, Fionn, have every warrior ready for what might come out.'

It had taken Fionn, the High King and several of the Fianna two nights of travelling to reach Rathcroghan. When they arrived, the Chief Druid had told them of that fateful day's events. How Cana had stayed behind to hold back the monsters that were being released, giving Caicer the precious time he needed to close the portal stone. Lughnasa had passed and nothing had been heard since of the Dealra Dubh and its Otherworldly army. But nothing had been heard of Cana either.

Caicer read from the Great Book of Moytura as Tadg had done only a few weeks previously, and once again the portal slid open. But inside, they found nothing. The bridge was gone. Disappeared. And so was any other sign that a conflict had taken place. As for Cana, nothing. No clues, no sign, no scent.

An hour later they were outside again, looking at the Rathcroghan sidhe, where Fionn had first lost Sadb and now Cana, the two people he loved more than any in this world.

'Well?' Art asked.

'Close it up, High King,' Fionn answered. 'Bury everything.'

As the entrance to the sidhe was submerged under a hundred tons of rock and soil, Caicer spoke to Fionn about what Diorraing had seen in the sidhe – how a great brown bear had emerged with eyes like Créde's. 'Tadg had cast a spell on her, expecting that her Tuatha ancestors were half-owl, hare or ...'

'Deer?' Fionn asked.

'Yes, or deer,' said Caicer. 'He didn't know that Créde's grandfather was Artio, a Tuatha half-bear half-man.'

'Who was Sadb's father?' Fionn asked.

'Cernunnos, half a horned stag, half a human, master of wild places and things.'

'So that day on the beach, when Cnes spotted the strange sight of a deer being chased by our hounds ...?'

'Yes, I believe that was Sadb. I should have known when Cnes first shared the story but I – I'm sorry.'

Fionn swallowed bitterly.

There was a knock at the door. 'Iollan, you here?'

Clean-shaven and well-clothed, Iollan answered it. 'Hi, Fionn, just give me a moment.'

A full year had passed since Goll and Tadg's failed invasion and Lughnasa had swung round again. However, this year it was following a brighter tradition: the trial-marriage ceremonies of several Fianna warriors were about to take place.

'Nervous?' Fionn asked.

'A little,' said Iollan. 'Cnes's father Lochan called in early today and told me what would happen if I didn't treat her well.'

'What did he say?' Fionn asked.

'That I would have to answer to Cnes!' Both friends laughed. 'How do I look?'

'Clean.'

Fionn grinned, reminded of a past conversation.

'Is everyone ready?' asked Iollan.

'Yes. The High King and Chief Druid are standing ready to begin the ceremony. Eitne has helped create some amazing food, but don't worry, we haven't let her near the soup. Connla and Covey have been busy all week readying a pack of wolfhounds as a guard of honour. And Cailte has a few new songs ready.'

'And the others?'

'Well, Ernamis rode in yesterday evening, with Crimmal. Donn and Lugach are looking particularly smart. While Sárait looks ...'

'Ferocious?'

'Ferociously happy.' Fionn smiled. 'Anyway, I'll leave you to get ready and will see you out there.'

'Fionn, how are you feeling?'

'I'm okay. Delighted for you and Cnes and hopeful that you will survive your year and a day of marriage and make it permanent.'

'Don't forget Diorraing and Ossnat too,' Iollan added. 'They're marrying today as well, after all.'

'Yes, I know. I'm not worried for them, though. Their idea of romance is for Diorraing to carry Ossnat out of a dark cave to safety. Half the time, I think you and Cnes would like to put each other in one!'

Iollan smiled. 'I know — isn't she great? What of you? With Goll and Tadg defeated, and a Fianna to be proud of, what are your plans?'

'After the ceremonies, I'll ride to Ulster to renew our northern defences. Come winter, I might travel to the mount of Ben Bulben in Sligeach. Reports came to me some weeks back of a strange solitary deer.'

'Sadb?'

'Who knows, but I won't stop looking for her — for both her and Cana.'

Iollan nodded. 'You know, there are other people you might meet.'

Fionn smiled once more and gave a quick whistle. In bounded Conbec, all hind legs and fur, jumping into Fionn's arms and sending him to the floor. 'Don't worry — I'm not alone. And to be honest, I don't think I ever will be.'

# ACKNOWLEDGEMENTS

In researching this book, I spent many, many hours reading the *Transactions of the Ossianic Society* — a body of publications written more than 160 years ago by a few individuals interested in the preservation and publication of ancient Irish manuscripts, in which the stories of Fionn Mac Cumhaill were first recorded. From these publications, as well as more modern translations, such as Ann Dooley and Harry Roe's *Acallam na Senórach*, I have received much of the inspiration that has helped to fill the pages of this book.

I want to thank my parents-in-law, Anne-Marie Quinn and Richard Haworth, for their knowledge, advice and wisdom, as well as my own parents, Teresa and Danny, for their constant love and support. Thanks again to Max and Juliet for their insights.

Finally, I am indebted to Deirdre, Aoibheann and the rest of the team at Gill Books for their help.

# ABOUT THE AUTHOR
## AND ILLUSTRATOR

RONAN MOORE is an author and secondary-school English teacher whose storytelling is thankfully a lot better than his spelling. As well as trying to help young adults see the world in a different light, he enjoys running — both on the road and after his kids. He lives in Meath with his wife and three children.

ALEXANDRA COLOMBO is an illustrator from Bulgaria. She attended the Milan European Institute of Design and received a first-class degree in Illustration. Her great passion is writing and illustrating poems, books and fairy tales.